NO MAN'S LAND

uclanpublishing

No Man's Land is a uclanpublishing book

First published in Great Britain in 2021 by
uclanpublishing
University of Central Lancashire
Preston, PR1 2HE, UK

First published in the UK 2021

Text copyright © Joanna Nadin 2021
Illustrated by Lucy Mulligan
Designed by Amy Cooper

'Fascism: I sometimes fear . . .' by Michael Rosen. First published in
Don't Mention the Children by Michael Rosen (Smokestack Books, 2015)

978-1912979-61-5

1 3 5 7 9 10 8 6 4 2

Set in 12/19.5pt Kingfisher by Amy Cooper

A CIP catalogue record for this book is available from the British Library.

Printed and bound in Great Britain by Clays Ltd, Elcograf S.p.A.

NO MAN'S LAND

For the real Sam,
and his brother Gabriel

I sometimes fear that
people think that fascism arrives in fancy dress
worn by grotesques and monsters
as played out in endless re-runs of the Nazis.

Fascism arrives as your friend.
It will restore your honour,
make you feel proud,
protect your house,
give you a job,
clean up the neighbourhood,
remind you of how great you once were,
clear out the venal and corrupt,
remove anything you feel is unlike you . . .

It doesn't walk in saying,
"Our programme means militias, mass imprisonments,
transportations, war and persecution."

'Fascism: I sometimes fear. . .' by Michael Rosen

PART 1: ALBION

HEROES AND VILLAINS

I used to think I knew about heroes. That some wore fancy outfits and flexed bulging muscles and had special powers like invisibility or flight or flames from their fingertips. The others wore uniforms and fought for the country with guns and rockets, or carried babies out of burning buildings.

It turns out not all heroes wear capes. And not all heroes carry guns.

It turns out it's not so easy to tell them and the baddies apart, neither.

'Cause real life isn't like on the telly or in films. Villains don't always go round cackling madly and flashing their tattoos. They come in pretending to be your friend and promising you stuff so you're tricked into thinking they're the good ones after all.

And the real heroes? They can slip in and out without you even noticing. And fight with their wile and their wits and their kindness instead of weapons.

And they might be skinny as a stick and dressed in a T-shirt and just a kid.

But I didn't know that then.

I just knew the world was changing.

And I knew I wanted it to stop.

HOW IT BEGAN

It started with Mrs King.

Actually, that's not totally true. It started ages ago when the Albioneers won the election. Maybe before, even – before I was born. When England decided it didn't like Europe any more and then there was graffiti on the Co-op wall telling anyone who wasn't white, or the right kind of white, to go home, even though home was here. Then home changed its name anyway, turned into Albion, and it wasn't the same for any of us.

That's what Dad would say, anyway. But Dad wasn't around for half the story, and he's not telling it, I am. So I say it started with Mrs King.

Least for Sam and me.

FRANZ FERDINAND

She'd been teaching us about World War One, and the soldiers in the trenches whose feet got rotten, and the rats as big as cats that tried to eat the dead bodies. Ahmed said the soldiers should've eaten the rats, and Jayden Nesbitt said he *would* say that, so Ahmed said, 'What's that supposed to mean?'

Jayden said, 'You know what that means,' and called him a dirty word.

And Mrs King said that was enough and that no one ate anyone and that this kind of attitude was how world wars started. So Ahmed said actually she'd said some man called Franz Ferdinand getting shot was what started the war.

Mrs King said, 'Not "some man". He was the

Archduke, Ahmed. And Franz Ferdinand was just the tipping point. The arguing was the build-up. Wars don't come from nowhere.'

And then no one spoke for a bit and the air in the room felt fat and dangerous because we all knew war might be coming again. It'd been on the news. We weren't allowed news in our house because of most of it being fake, but Ahmed told me, so I knew too. Sam didn't; he was only five and he mainly cared about Marvel and DC and dinosaurs, but I was ten and old enough for truth, least I thought so. Like I knew Cassius Barker from our class hadn't moved school, he'd been sent to his uncle in Trinidad because it was safer there. And I knew that Olivia Mikkelsen who used to work with Dad at Albion Interception had gone back to Denmark. And I knew that the Patels from number forty-four had gone to Bangladesh and all.

And I knew that the war wouldn't be loud and clattering with guns and bombs and trenches this time, it would be stealthy and silent and sneak in at night when you weren't expecting it.

It was confusing, too: who was good and who was bad, and whose side was I meant to be on – Albion's side, or The Rest of the World's. I'd asked Dad to explain it and he said it was more complicated than that and that there were good people and bad people in all the countries, and some people even had good and bad inside them, and to just to get on with being a kid, maybe, for a bit.

Finally, Mrs King smiled, wide and real. She said we'd probably done enough war for the day and we should get on with painting our mural of Important Women, which was of a scientist called Marie Curie and a writer called Maya Angelou and a girl called Rosa Parks who had sat in the wrong bit of the bus, which was brave because she was black. So we did.

Only, Ahmed and Jayden argued about where Ahmed should sit on the bus, which Jayden said was in the driver's seat and Ahmed said was in the bus company headquarters, owning all the buses in the world. And Mrs King was just telling them to pack it in when Paris Metcalfe from next door spilt pink paint all over her shoes, and started crying because they were expensive and her mum would kill her, and Mrs King said she'd clean them up so they were as good as new, and by the time she was done they almost were.

Then it was home time and she said, 'Goodbye, everyone, see you all tomorrow!' like she always does. And I didn't even say bye back and nor did anyone else because we were too pleased to get out and play football or cricket or just eat crisps or whatever.

But I should have; we all should. Because, even though we didn't realise it at the time, Mrs King was our tipping point. She was our Franz Ferdinand.

Because the next day, she was gone.

MR GOSFORTH

The mural had gone and all.

Instead, there was just a big blank wall with holes where the pins had been, and standing in front was the head teacher Mrs Pritchard looking a bit sick and a tall man with a red face and grey hair called Mr Gosforth, which I knew because he'd written it on the whiteboard and underlined it twice in case we might not remember it or realise it was important.

'Any questions?' said Mrs Pritchard, and Ahmed stuck his hand right up.

'Where's Mrs King?' he said.

'She's unable to teach at the moment,' said Mrs Pritchard. Only when she said 'unable', her voice went weird like Dad's did when he said he was fine that time after playing football and it turned out he'd fractured a leg and had to go into hospital and Horrible Nan had to look after us for a week – i.e. it was a lie.

Paris's hand went up. 'What's wrong with her?'

'I . . . I don't know,' said Mrs Pritchard in that weird voice again.

'When's she coming back?' said Paris, and this time she didn't have her hand up, which usually means you lose five minutes of golden time, which is when you can choose to do anything you want, even games, but Mrs Pritchard must have forgotten.

'I don't know,' she said again, and this time it wasn't a lie, but it wasn't good either. 'Any questions not about Mrs King?'

I put up my hand. 'Where's our mural gone?'

This time Mr Gosforth answered. 'It was deemed inappropriate,' he said.

Which no one understood, which he must've realised because then he added, 'Not suitable.'

'Why?' I asked.

'Did I call on you?' said Mr Gosforth to me. 'No,' he continued. 'Five minutes gone.' Then he turned to Mrs Pritchard. 'I can take it from here,' he said.

Mrs Pritchard smiled. But it was the kind of smile that actually means 'I'm not happy about this at all', which is Horrible Nan's main kind. Then she left.

Immediately, everyone was whispering madly about Mrs King and why she'd gone and where she was and what was going on, then Mr Gosforth clapped his hands so hard it sounded like a crack and it sent dust dancing into the sunlight and silence.

No one moved a muscle. No one said a word.

'Right then,' said Mr Gosforth. 'Maths.'

THEORIES

After school me and Ahmed walked Sam back to mine and Paris Metcalfe came too because of having to be chaperoned, which means watched over, because of being a girl. Normally we talk about e.g. who would win in a fight: Spider-Man or a Megalosaurus, which Sam always says is the Megalosaurus and Ahmed always says is Spider-Man and Paris always says is just stupid and made-up and who cares anyway? But that day, we were all deciding what had happened to Mrs King.

'It'll be a sick bug,' said Ahmed, sounding like he knew what he was talking about. 'Forty-eight-hour thing.'

'Shows what you know,' said Paris.

'I do know,' said Ahmed.

'What, 'cause your dad's a doctor?'

'Yeah. So?'

'I was sick,' said Sam. 'On Helen.'

Helen is one of his plastic dinosaurs. The other two are James and Wolverine.

'When?' Paris edged away from him.

'On my birthday,' said Sam. 'It was all cake.'

Paris sighed then 'cause Sam's birthday was months ago. 'Anyway,' she carried on. 'It's probably 'cause she's a Traitor.'

'Helen's a Traitor?' I said.

'No, duh. Mrs King.'

Ahmed stopped. I stopped. Even Sam stopped. 'What's a Traitor?' he said.

'Someone against the king and Albion,' I said. 'And anyway, she's not.'

'How do you know?' Paris stuck her hands on her hips.

'Well, how do *you*?' replied Ahmed. 'You think everyone's a Traitor. Just because your dad's an Albioneer.'

Paris's dad wasn't just any old Albioneer, he was

a massive one, in charge of local rallies and stuff. And he was massive in other ways, too. Like, his neck was wider than his head and his arms were as big as our dad's thighs and on one of them he had a tattoo saying AAA for Albion-America Alliance, which was who was wanting war against The Rest of the World.

Her mum looked almost normal though. Just like any mum, I suppose, with earrings and leggings and lipstick. Still, we had to be careful. Even though she was always saying 'call me Donna' and handing out mini Mars bars or rocket lollies over the fence, because 'someone has to take care of you boys.' Because of us not having a mum. Which isn't even true. We did have one, but she died having Sam. It's Not His Fault though. I know that because Dad told me every day for a year and always in capitals. Until he actually believed it.

'Did you hear me?' said Ahmed. 'I said it's just because your dad's an Albioneer.'

Paris pulled a face. 'Whatever. Anyway, I could report you for that.'

'Go on then.'

'I will then.' And Paris stomped off by herself, which was against the Guidelines, but it was only about four houses, so was probably OK.

'You shouldn't have said that,' I told Ahmed. 'What if she does?'

Ahmed shrugged. 'What's she going to tell him? That I'm not white? Reckon he can see that for himself.'

I felt a bit sick then. Because I *am* white. But that isn't my fault any more than not being is his and what did it matter anyway? 'Still,' I said.

'It'll be fine,' Ahmed said. 'Mrs King'll be back and all. Tomorrow, probably. You'll see.' And he nudged Sam. 'Who would win in a fight?' he said then. 'Megalosaurus or Mr Metcalfe?'

But I still felt sick, because I could feel it coming. War, I mean. Creeping up on us, into our town, down our street, into our house. Smiling like a friend, like it was Batman come to save us when really it was the Joker all along.

THE LIST

Mrs King wasn't back the next day. Or the day after that, or the day after that.

'Definitely a Traitor,' said Paris. 'Maybe even Resistance.' She whispered that word – *Resistance* – because no one dared say it too loud, because of who might be listening, but it felt dangerous and dirty all the same.

Resistance was the worst kind of Traitor, according to Albioneers. Not just against Albion like the Traitors, but plotting to stop it, to use their own guns and stuff to go back to how things used to be, before all of this. And that was confusing too because in World War Two, the Resistance were the goodies. Only now, you had to hate them.

'She is not,' I snapped. 'How can she be?'

Resistance were men, weren't they?

'Not what I heard,' Paris carried on. 'I heard Albion's rounding them up. I heard there's a list with addresses on.'

My stomach jumped at that, even though I knew we definitely weren't Resistance. 'What addresses?' I asked, suddenly seeing our house, seeing '11 Bentley Street' typed out with a red cross next to it.

'None of your business,' she said.

'You don't know anything,' said Ahmed. 'You're making it up, as usual.' But even he didn't sound sure any more.

'War's coming whether you like it or not,' Paris said then, all matter of fact. 'It was on the news. Europe has to back down or else.'

'Or else what?' said Sam.

'Duh, have you been listening? War.'

'Oi,' I said. 'Don't have a go at him. He's only five.'

'And nearly seven months,' he added.

'Whatever.' Paris shrugged. 'I'll be safe though. Albion'll have our backs, Dad says. 'Cause of him signing up to fight.'

'Fighting who?' I asked, only quiet this time.

'Oh my GOD. Fighting The Rest of the World!' She said it like it was a triumph, then eyed me and Sam up and down. 'Who'll have you?' she asked then.

'What do you mean, "who'll have us"?' I asked, sort of jokily. Though I didn't feel it. I felt odd and bothered.

'When your dad signs up. Unless he's not going to,' she said, the words all poky like a stick. 'Unless he's a Traitor and all.'

I felt my face get hot and looked at Sam quick, but he was busy with his dinosaurs so I looked back at Paris, who was waiting with one hand on her hip and one twirling a Chupa Chups as if she was a princess. 'Our dad is NOT a Traitor,' I spat. 'He works at Albion Interception, doesn't he? That's, like, practically the government!'

'Then he'll sign up, won't he?' She shrugged. 'You could come and live with me, only I'll probably go to my nan's. She's in the Forest of Dene and, like my dad says, who'd bomb that?'

Horrible Nan popped into my head, all thin lips and lemon-bitter.

'You could come to ours,' said Ahmed.

Paris smirked. 'As if they'll let you stay.' Then she turned back to me, her smile wide as a crocodile's. ''Course, it'd be different if you had a mum.'

And I didn't say anything to that, not one single word. And nor did Ahmed. And nor did Sam.

Because we all knew she was right.

CODE

I like code. Because you don't have to be a Chosen One or have superpowers like e.g. melting death-rays to work it out. You just need patience and concentration.

Maybe not the kind of code that Dad works in, which is intercepting messages from countries that are against Albion. You have to be pretty special for that. More like Alan Turing, the code-breaker who solved the German messages with their sneaky Enigma machines and helped end World War Two, and is how I got my name. I can't do that sort of thing, not yet. But I can do the everyday kind. Because code is everywhere if you think about it. Foreign languages are a kind of code. Abbreviations are a kind of code. Even emojis are a kind of code. Like me and Ahmed use the pig one for Paris and the poo one for Jayden Nesbitt.

Me and Dad had our own code and all. For instance, on his way out in the morning he'd say, 'Elvis has left the building.' And when he got in, he'd say, 'The Eagle has landed.' And he's not Elvis or an eagle, but in our code, he's both.

Only, not today. Today when he got in what he said was, 'Why the long face? Feeling Tom and Dick?'

Long face means sad. And Tom and Dick means sick. Only I wasn't sad. Or sick. Not the throwing-up-on-a-plastic-dinosaur kind anyway.

Just scared.

'Is it true?' I said. 'Is war coming? Only, Paris says it is and that they're rounding people up. Traitors and Resistance. There's a list.'

'Hold your horses, mate,' Dad said then. Which is our code for slow down.

'Her dad's going to fight,' added Sam. 'With a gun. Or antibiotic-resistant bacteria. Or another virus. That's how the world will end. Mr Hinckley said so.'

'Cheery,' said Dad. And he smiled, to show he wasn't bothered about bacteria, but the smile was like Mrs Pritchard's from before.

'Will we have to go to Horrible Nan's?' I asked straight out.

'What? No,' said Dad. 'And don't call her that.'

'*You* don't even like her,' Sam said, which was true. Because she was Mum's mum and didn't think Dad was dad material, or even husband material, only luckily Mum hadn't agreed or we wouldn't even be here. 'Is she a Traitor?' Sam added.

'What?' Dad blurted. 'No—'

'Is she Resistance then?' Sam carried on. 'What even *is* Resistance? Are *we* Resistance?'

Dad's mouth was hanging open like he might catch flies.

'Sam,' I warned. Only not that loud, because I wanted to know too.

Dad closed his mouth at last and shook his head. 'No. I—'

'So who is?' I asked. 'The French again?'

Dad shook his head again. 'It's not like World War Two, Alan,' he explained. 'The Germans . . . they're not the baddies any more.'

'Are we the baddies?' asked Sam.

'No!' Dad said, loud and definite. 'Not us three, anyway. It's hard to explain. Albion's kind of bad, but—'

'So why d'you work for them?' I demanded.

'Because that's what I'm good at. And . . . I didn't choose to work for Albion. There was another government before that. They're weren't so . . . strict.'

'So what *are* we, then?' I said. 'If we're not Albion and we're not Resistance and we're not the . . . villains.'

'Are we the heroes?' Sam added, excited now. 'Are we?'

Even I was excited. Because what if we *were* the heroes? What if we were going to fix everything? I didn't know how, but perhaps we were Chosen Ones and we just didn't know it yet. Perhaps we'd discover superpowers, or a Batmobile in the bunker. Or—

'We're just . . . ordinary people,' Dad said, swiping

my shiny idea right out of the air like it was just a fly, 'caught up in the middle of it all.'

'Oh,' said Sam, disappointed.

'How about a game?' Dad said then. 'Or a film?'

'*Iron Man*,' said Sam.

And Dad said yes, even though we'd watched it seven times in a month and last time he'd said he'd rather chew his own eyeballs out than watch it again.

That's how I knew even Dad was worried. Because he didn't bellyache, which is our code for complain.

He didn't say anything at all.

Not through tea, which was sausages and spaghetti hoops, which is only Sam's third best and he said so. Not afterwards, when Sam knocked his milk all over the carpet because of pretending to be Hulk. Not even when Sam refused to have a bath in case good bacteria got washed off him and got replaced with antibiotic-resistant ones.

It wasn't until we were in bed and I heard Dad murmur and I knew he was on the phone then and I guessed it was Billy Ringman, codename

'Ringo', who's his mate and who works at AI as well. And mainly they talk about work and football and whether Dave's wife Jeanie is unreasonable or not. And mostly I try not to listen in case it's 'NSFC' which is code for Not Suitable for Children.

Only, tonight I needed a glass of water because of too much salt on the fish fingers, which Dad is always telling me off for but he hadn't this time. So I crept to the top of the stairs and that's when I heard it. It wasn't Dave he was talking to. It wasn't even 'Ringo'.

'It's time, Julia,' said Dad. 'It's time.'

MUM

I don't remember much about Mum because I was only five when she died so I had to keep a List. A real one on paper, not just in my head. Then every time I found something out about her, I added it on. So far there were ten things on it:

1. That she had longish reddy-brown hair and freckles (like me, only my hair's short) and a dimple in her right cheek when she smiled.

2. That she knew all the words to every song that ever came on the radio but her favourite was 'Heroes' by a man called David Bowie, and if that ever comes on the radio now Dad switches it off.

3. That she smelt of lemons.

4.   That sometimes she smoked cigarettes, which Horrible Nan said would be the death of her, only they weren't in the end, but no one has dared point that out to Horrible Nan.

5.   That her best tea was spaghetti bolognese and her worst was fish fingers but she still ate them because they were my best tea.

6.   That she was allergic to cats, dogs, rabbits and horses so we never had a pet, not even a fish or a hamster, just in case.

7.   That she went to boarding school, and it was only girls there, and they had to wear hats, and she hated it. Which is why Dad said it would be over his dead body when Horrible Nan said it might be an idea to send me and Sam to one.

8.   That she was even better at code than Dad, which is why she was his boss, which is how they met.

9.   That once she got stung by a jellyfish on her foot and Dad weed on it (the foot not the jellyfish) because they'd read that it stopped

the hurting, only that turned out to be a big pork pie, which means lie, so then she had a smelly foot as well as being in agony.

10. That she was the one who rescued me when I got stuck in the bunker. The bunker is a room under the kitchen that got built for another war – a nuclear one that never came – only now the way in is shut and under a rug and Sam doesn't even know about it and Dad says it had better stay that way.

But then I remembered something else. I remembered that when Mum died, after Dad had stopped crying, he said he had to call 'Julia', even before he called Horrible Nan.

That's how I knew Julia wasn't a code. Julia was real. And if Dad was calling her, something was definitely wrong. So even though I had a new memory like a gem to write down under number 11, I couldn't be happy. Not properly. Not until I knew what was going on.

JULIA

'Why did you call Julia?' I asked at breakfast, which was Coco Pops, which we're not normally allowed on a weekday but Dad hadn't had time to do the shopping so it was that or baked beans and Sam won't eat baked beans, not even in a sandwich, which is how he has to eat anything weird so he can't see it.

'Who's Julia?' said Sam.

'No one,' said Dad.

'Yes she is,' I said.

'Not now,' said Dad. 'And you shouldn't have been earwigging.' Which means listening. But that wasn't the point and I said so.

'No arguments!' snapped Dad.

Sam stopped chewing at that because Dad never

snaps, not unless something massive has happened e.g. like the time Sam tried to turn the bath into a Lazarus Pit like the one that healed Batman, only he used up all the washing-up liquid and a whole carton of chocolate milk and two bottles of Dad's beer and it just looked like bin juice anyway.

'Sorry,' Dad said. 'Just, I'll tell you later.'

'Later when?' I asked.

'I don't know. After school maybe.'

I'd stopped chewing and all by then because my stomach was hard and tight as a cricket ball. 'I don't want to go to school,' I said. 'I don't feel well.'

Dad looked at me like he knew I was lying, which I wasn't, not properly. 'I don't have time for this,' he said. 'You're going to school, and then you're coming straight home, OK? No dawdling. And no Ahmed. Not today.'

'What's going on?'

'I said I'd tell you later.'

'You're never even home when we get back anyway,' said Sam, which was true.

'Paris says we might as well be orphans,' I added.

'Oh, for God's sake,' said Dad. 'And I'll be back today so just . . . do as I say, all right?'

***

And we did. We went to school. And Mr Gosforth made our class do Henry the Eighth instead of Rosa Parks, because Henry the Eighth was from Albion and white. And he didn't even put Jayden Nesbitt's name on the board when he said Henry should have chopped off Catherine of Aragon's head as well as Anne Boleyn's because of being Spanish and therefore probably a Traitor.

And on the way home, Paris banged on about the list again and Ahmed sent me a text of the pig emoji and the sick emoji, even though he was walking right next to me, and I smiled but I didn't laugh, and he said no worries about not coming round tonight 'cause I could go round his tomorrow and play *Doom* and Sam could come if he wanted. Which he did, because Dad never lets him play computer games at ours because his 'capacity for imagination is big enough already' i.e. Dad doesn't want him trying to turn the bathroom into an acid pool again.

And then Ahmed said, 'see you', just like Mrs King had, and I said, 'see you' back because I didn't want to make that mistake again.

But it wasn't enough. Because if I'd known what was about to happen, I'd have hugged him or something. If I'd known, I'd have gone round his right there and then and begged his mum to let me stay. If I'd known, I'd have begged anyone to let me stay.

Because when we got in Dad *was* home, which had only happened once before when he had flu so bad he was sick on himself in the shower, which I said was practical and Sam said was gross. But this time he wasn't being sick. He wasn't even coughing a bit.

He was standing in the front room with mine and Sam's suitcases from the time we went to Benidorm to see Nice Nan.

And that's when I realised about Mrs King being our Franz Ferdinand. Because I knew right then that everything was about to change.

EVACUATION

The thing about Sam is, he'll do anything if you tell him it's a game. Literally anything. Me and Ahmed used to test it sometimes. 'Eat this slightly mouldy orange, Sam,' I'd say. And he'd say, 'Why?' and I'd say, 'It's a game.' 'OK,' he'd say, and he would. And he shut himself in the airing cupboard for half an hour, and went to school in wellies and did a wee in the bath, all for a game, which is when Dad found out and said we had to stop because it was mean. I said it wasn't that mean because Sam was having fun but Dad said pretending something was a game when it wasn't was a lie and lies were always bad.

This time, though, it was Dad who was the bad one.

'What's going on?' I asked, eyeing the cases.

Dad shifted, which is a sort of body code for being guilty. You don't even know your body's doing code but it is. Like when you lie, you fidget, or touch your face or look up to the left. For truth it's down to the right.

Dad did not look down to the right.

'You're going away,' he said. 'Just for a little bit.'

'Going where?' asked Sam. 'Is it holiday? Is it Benidorm? Will I be sick again?' Because last time he was sick on the plane and had to wear his pants for the rest of the flight.

'No,' said Dad. 'Not Benidorm.'

'Florida?' tried Sam. Because he's desperate to go to Florida ever since his friend Mason went and saw an actual live crocodile. Dad said we could see one in Brigstowe Zoo but even Sam said it wasn't the same.

'Sorry, Sam,' said Dad. 'Not Florida.'

'Where then?' I said. And I thought I might be the one being sick then, because my stomach was a swirling soup. 'Is it . . .' I remembered Olivia

Mikkelsen, and Cassius Barker, and the Patels. 'Is it Bangladesh?'

'Is it?' Sam asked, his voice fat with panic. 'Will we have to eat curry?' Because he hates curry. Even korma, which isn't even hot. Even in a sandwich.

'Don't be daft,' said Dad, picking up Sam and rubbing him. 'Why would you be going there?'

That was the second time he'd said 'you' not 'we' and now it was my head swirling, all dizzy and quick. 'Because . . . Because of the war?' I said.

Sam lifted his head off Dad's shoulder. 'Is it war now?' he asked through his snot.

'No,' Dad said, shifting again. 'It's . . . think of it like a game.'

And I knew then it was a lie and not even a white one, but a big fat whopper. But Sam was happy, and that was what mattered to Dad.

'A game! A game!' Sam sang to himself.

'That's right,' said Dad. 'A secret location. So you have to pack, OK?'

'Pack what?' I snapped. 'Swimming trunks?' Which was sarcasm, which was another sort of grown-up lie.

Dad fixed me with a look like a 'please'. 'If you like,' he said.

I looked away, at the fridge with the magnets that spelt 'Sam smells' and 'Alan is best'. 'You know school doesn't finish for another two days,' I told him then.

'I don't think missing two days of school will kill you, eh?'

Sam shook his head and wriggled down off Dad before belting upstairs.

I scowled. 'You know he'll just pack his dinosaurs and a Batman suit.'

'So let him,' said Dad. 'You'll be sensible, though. Won't you?' And his face was another please, a desperate one, so I had to say yes, didn't I?

'It's not Horrible Nan's, is it?' I asked then.

'No,' said Dad. 'It's not Horrible Nan's.'

That was good. But the soup was still churning in me.

'Is it far?'

'Just a drive away.'

That was good too. But not good enough.

'And you're not coming, are you,' I blurted. 'You said "you" not "we".'

'Clever kid,' Dad said. Which usually felt sweet as syrup but not today.

Perhaps it was better not to be clever. Perhaps I'd be happy as Sam if I didn't understand stuff. 'Why not?'

'I have to work,' Dad said. And he said it so quick I could tell it was true.

'But . . . Is it . . . Is it for ever?' I stammered.

Dad shook his head. 'No, Al. I . . . At least until things have calmed down. You understand, don't you? It's . . . it's just to be safe.'

I nodded. I did understand because we'd done evacuation at school last year, when we had Mr Potts who smelt of dog. 'But what about my birthday?' I remembered. Because we were supposed to go to the trampoline park for that – me and Sam and Ahmed as well. Dad had promised. 'Will you fetch us back for that?'

Dad thought for a minute and I knew he was trying to remember when it was, which was in just over two weeks, in August, which was on the calendar so he didn't forget like he did one year. Eventually he nodded. 'For your birthday.'

And even though I didn't really believe him, I grabbed that like it was a magic talisman and held on to it hard, so hard my fingers hurt.

'OK then,' I said. 'I'll pack.'

PACKING

I was sensible in the end. I packed important things like the four-leaf clover in plastic that Nice Nan had given me once for luck, and my seventeen best Batman comics, and my List. But practical things too. Useful things. Like my wellies, and my torch, and my penknife that has eleven gadgets on it, even scissors.

And all the while, I wondered where it might be that we were going. It had to be somewhere safe, so not Europe because of the war. And not Glasgu where Aunty Jeanie lived, because Caledonia was too far to drive even though it was Independent, i.e. not in cahoots with Albion. And not Caerdyff where Uncle Tom lived, because Wealas was definitely in cahoots with Albion. So if Albion wasn't safe, nor was Wealas.

But when he came up to say good night, Dad still wouldn't tell me where.

'Just promise it's not Bangladesh,' I said.

'Christ on a bike,' Dad said. 'What's with Bangladesh all of a sudden?'

'The Patels went,' I said. 'And it's really far.'

'Well, you're not,' Dad replied. 'I couldn't afford it even I wanted to. And I don't.'

'The Patels afforded it,' I muttered. 'And their house was smaller than ours.'

Dad sighed. 'They didn't pay though, did they. Albion did.'

I thought of Ahmed then, and if Albion was going to pay to send him and his mum and dad and sisters somewhere and all and I must've gone quiet because then Dad said, 'Everything will be fine. It'll all be back to normal before you know it.'

But he'd said that when Mum went into hospital to have Sam and look what happened. I didn't say anything about that though. I just asked, 'Are we going in the morning?'

Dad nodded. 'Bright and early.'

'How early?'

'Early enough that you need to turn your light off in the next five minutes. And I'll have your phone now.'

'But—'

'No buts,' said Dad, taking it off me and putting it in his pocket. 'Not tonight.'

I sighed because I hadn't texted Ahmed yet and crossed my arms.

'You're a trooper,' Dad told me then. 'A real little hero.'

I felt weird at that. 'You said we aren't the heroes. You said we're just ordinary—'

'I didn't mean that kind of hero,' Dad snapped. Then, 'Sorry,' he added, quick sharp. 'Just that . . . your mum would be proud.'

And I knew then it was big and I knew he meant it, because he never mentioned Mum, not if he could help it.

'Thanks,' I said.

But after he'd gone, I didn't take out the List

and I didn't write what he'd said down under number 12.

Because I wasn't a hero. Not any kind.

Because that was when I still thought heroes could do things like melt aeroplanes or fight vampires or stop time. Or they flew helicopters and steered submarines and gunned down the enemy.

Heroes saved people and I'd already lost Mum.

What if I lost Dad and all?

THE ALARM

It was definitely early when Dad woke us. So early it was still pitch-black out.

I looked at my glow-in-the-dark alarm clock. 2:15, it said in luminous green. I groaned and turned over, but Dad yanked back the duvet.

'Come on, kid,' he said. 'It's time.'

And soon as he'd said it, I was awake, more awake than I'd ever been, my eyes wide and my insides jittering like they had insects in them.

'Don't worry about that,' Dad said when I went to do my teeth.

He'd never said that before, not once.

'Come on,' he urged.

'All right,' I said. 'Keep your hair on.' Which means calm down and is a code and a joke in one, because Dad is a bit bald at the back. Only it didn't feel funny right then, and neither of us smiled. 'Where's Sam?' I said.

'Asleep,' Dad said. 'I'll have to carry him. Just get the cases, will you?'

'Why is it so early?' I asked as I hauled the cases across the hall.

'Just because,' said Dad. Which is code for 'stop asking questions'.

But I had one left. 'Can I have my phone?' I asked.

'Why?'

'To text Ahmed.'

'No phones,' said Dad.

The insects in me flapped their wings. 'What?'

'I can't . . . I can't explain, but it's for the best.'

'But—' My head was racing. 'I promised. I said to him I'd walk to school with him. He won't know where I am. He won't—'

'Not now, please,' begged Dad. 'I'll sort something, all right. Just . . . not right now, Alan.'

He'd said my name. Not just 'Al' but all of it, to show he meant business.

So I just trudged to the door, dragging the cases behind me, to show I meant business as well.

Because I had to be big, didn't I. I had to get into the car. I had to strap myself in. I had to wait while Sam, mouth gaping in his sleep like a baby bird, got strapped in. And all of it quiet as you like, so no one beaked at us out their window and clocked us leave.

The thing was, I'd waited ages for something like this. For something to happen to me like it happens to Superman or Hulk or Thor. Something secret and big and brilliant, even if it was scary. But now it was happening, I just felt sick and scared and wished everything could stay like it was.

Because this was Albion and everything was changing. And not for the better, whatever the Metcalfes said.

I looked up with a start when I thought that, checked the Metcalfes' windows for earwiggers. But nosy old Paris must have been asleep, and her mum and Mr Metcalfe too because the house was dark and the curtains closed and still, not twitching.

That was something, I thought, as the car rolled quietly down our drive, over the weeds and the cracks and the bicycle bell that I'd still not brought in even though Dad had asked me three times.

Then past the garden where we'd climbed the dead apple tree and Sam had fractured his hand falling out of it.

Past the wall where me and Ahmed had to sit and watch Paris roller-skate when her mum was having a lie-down.

Past the corner shop where Mum used to buy me liquorice laces that turned our tongues black – number 12! For definite this time!

Then round the corner and away from Albion. Away from life as we knew it. And off to somewhere safe.

So why didn't I feel it?

THE TRIP

We were out of the city in minutes and heading south, that much I knew. But Dad hadn't got the satnav on so where exactly we were heading was still a mystery.

'Why can't we use it?' I asked.

'The satnav?' Dad's eyes met mine in the mirror.

I nodded.

'In case.'

'In case what?' But I got it before he told me. 'In case they check the history on it.'

'Clever kid,' said Dad again.

'So how do you know where we're going?'

'Because I've been there before,' Dad said.

'When?'

'Just . . . before.'

Before me? Before Mum? Before Albion?

'I might need your help though,' Dad added.

I knew he was changing the subject, but I also knew he had to. 'What sort of help?'

'Map-reading.'

'I'll need to sit in the front?' I tried.

Dad met my eyes again. 'Go on then,' he said. 'But not 'til you've had a sleep, mind.'

'I won't sleep.'

''Course you won't,' said Dad.

＊

I woke up just gone four according to my watch. In front of us the sky was inky still but behind, thin light sneaked over the horizon. The car was stopped; the engine was on, but no headlamps and nothing around us but woods.

'Where are we?' I asked.

Dad looked up. 'Not far,' he said. 'This is where I need you.'

I unclicked my seatbelt and climbed over the handbrake into the front. It's called 'shotgun' in code sometimes, that seat. Because of Americans and being able to shoot out the window while someone else drives.

I wasn't going to shoot anything though. Not ever.

I was just going to read a map.

'Here.' Dad pointed at the page.

I peered down but it was too blurry to make out so I got my torch out of my pocket.

'I knew you'd be sensible,' said Dad.

And I felt a flicker of warmth then, even though I was mainly pretending to be brave. To be a hero, like Dad wanted.

'Beeralston,' I said finally. 'What even *is* that?'

'It's a village,' Dad said. 'But we can't go through, we have to go round it.'

'Why?'

'Just . . . because,' Dad replied. 'Then down here, you see? To the river.'

'What's at the river?'

'You'll see. Just get me down there, OK?'

So I did. I got him down there, down deserted lanes into the thick of the woods and all the while with no lights on.

And then I saw it – the shimmer of the moon on water.

Dad stopped the engine.

The insects in me woke up.

'Before I wake Sam, I have to give you something.'

'Give me what?'

Dad reached into his coat pocket and pulled out a small slice of coloured plastic and a black block.

A credit card and a phone. The old-fashioned kind like Tony Stark had once. The kind used for secret calls and plotting and—

'For emergencies,' he said.

The first insect wings began to flap.

'What emergencies? Where's my old phone?'

'Back at home,' Dad said. 'You're to use this one now. This is safer.'

'Can I text Ahmed?' I asked.

Dad shook his head. 'No numbers in it but one.'

'Yours?'

Dad nodded. 'And you're to be clever, OK? No giving away where you are or who you're with.'

'Who *are* we with?'

Dad swallowed and nodded. 'Come and see,' he said. Then he clunked open the doors and, Sam in his arms again, stepped into the trees.

THE WOMEN

'Where are the men?' whispered Sam.

There were three people, standing there by the boat. Three women: one short and old, with hair to match; one about Dad's age with burgundy bunches; and a teenager with skin like milk in the moonlight and long pale hair like a mermaid or doll.

None of them men, none of them supposed to be out on their own like this. Not in Albion.

'No men,' said one of them to Sam. The old one. 'No need.'

Sam pulled a face, cupped his hand round Dad's ear. 'What if they're villains?' he whispered.

But they didn't look like villains. Not even the smiling kind. They didn't look like anyone I'd ever seen before.

'Come on,' said the burgundy one. 'You don't want to be hanging about.'

But I did, I wanted to hang about for as long as I could, holding on to Dad's hand like I was Sam's age, not nearly at secondary. Then I remembered school. Remembered Ahmed, who'd be waking up soon. Remembered Mr Gosforth who'd have to mark me absent – my first day off all year – so no certificate for me. Remembered Mrs King and wondered where she was right now.

Dad let go of my hand. 'Go on,' he said, nudging me forward.

I walked slowly, step by step by step, until I was close enough that the old one, who had a bit of moustache, could grab both bags and dump them in the boat. Maybe not as old as she looked, then.

'Get in,' she said. 'Sit down. I don't bite.'

I got in and sat down, though she looked like she might.

The burgundy one took Sam off Dad. 'We're going to be friends,' she said as she carried him aboard.

Sam looked at her. 'In the Game?'

She looked at Dad, who nodded. 'In the Game,' she repeated.

Dad was alone then. Standing there with nothing. And I wanted to go back to hug him, to cling on and not let him leave without me and all. But the old woman must've known because she sat me down and said not to move or I'd tip us all out and then where would we be? Drowned, that's what.

'I can swim,' I said.

'Sam can't,' Dad said quick.

'He'll be all right, Bill,' said Burgundy. 'You've done the right thing.'

'I know,' said Dad. Then he sort of shook himself into life. 'Right. Well, thanks, Julia.'

Julia! So that was her – Mum's friend.

'You don't need to thank me,' she said. 'Just look after yourself.'

Dad nodded. 'I will.'

Then he looked at me and for a moment I thought he was going to change his mind and grab me, and everything would go back to being safe. Or at least normal.

But he didn't. He just nodded at me, and then he turned and started back into the trees.

A sick feeling whooshed through me. 'August the second!' I called out. Loud – too loud because the girl shushed me with a skinny finger to her lips. But I didn't care because I needed to check.

Dad turned round, smiled thinly. 'I know,' he said. 'Just . . . look after Sam. And don't . . . don't try to be a hero, OK?'

I stared. 'OK,' I said.

'Promise?'

And I did, because I didn't get it, didn't know what I was promising. Not really. How could I even try to be a hero? I was just me.

Dad nodded. 'Good boy.'

Then he turned again and was gone.

For a second, the world sort of stopped and held its breath and it could've gone either way – we could have run, or screamed, or anything.

But then the girl plopped down beside me. 'I'm Poppy,' she said. 'This is my mum.' She nodded at Julia, who had Sam tight in her lap as he trailed one fat hand in the river. 'And that's Maggie.'

I looked at the old one again, who'd picked up the oars. 'Is she . . . is Maggie your nan?' I asked.

Poppy pulled a face. 'She's no one's nan,' she said, soft as the swish of an oar on water. 'But she's all right once you get used to her.'

'I heard that,' said Maggie, her voice low.

'You were supposed to,' said Poppy, nudging me and smiling.

And even though I didn't feel like it, I made my mouth smile too. Because sometimes if you do that it turns into a real one.

'Where are we going?' Sam asked then.

'Didn't your dad tell you?' asked Julia.

I shook my head.

'Only across the river,' said Poppy. 'Not far.'

I looked at the reedy bank and line of trees rising up behind it into a forest thicker than the one we'd come from. 'What's over there?' I asked.

Poppy smiled. 'That?' she said. 'That's No Man's Land.'

PART 2:
NO MAN'S LAND

THE FARM

It was a farm once, Julia said. Maggie and Julia's family had owned it – Maggie was Julia's aunt. Only, beef was cheaper from Europe and the farm had failed, and then Mr Minton – that was Maggie's brother, and Julia's uncle – had got ill and so Maggie had come back from Londinium and turned it into holiday homes.

It didn't look like holiday homes. Just a sprawl of cottages – empty, I reckoned – a falling down farmhouse, a few barns, and a long, low thing stacked out of fat slabs of grey. And all of them old – way older than our house.

'So, are there families?' asked Sam. 'With children?'

'Not really,' said Poppy. 'There's other women

– they come and go, and some of them have got kids.'

What women? I thought. But I didn't say anything. Not then.

'No one comes on holiday any more,' added Poppy. 'Not here, anyway.'

'Oh.' Sam sounded disappointed. 'You're not on holiday then?'

Poppy shook her head. 'We live here now. Moved twelve years ago. From Brigstowe.'

'Near us!' I blurted.

'Near you.' Julia smiled.

'So, no children.' Sam sighed.

'Except me,' said Poppy. 'And Noah.'

'Poppy's brother,' added Julia. 'Not that you'll see much of him. Fifteen and knows it all.'

'Does he actually?' asked Sam.

'Not even half,' replied Poppy. 'I know more than him and I'm twelve. Minnow's about your age though. She's six and the littlest. My half-sister,' she added.

'And Leon,' added Julia. 'Don't forget him.'

'And Leon.' Poppy nodded and her hair swished. 'He's Minnow's brother. But not from our mum. He's eighteen, only he might not seem it.'

'Why?' I asked.

'He's just ... Leon,' said Poppy. 'You'll understand when you meet him.'

'So there *are* men then,' I said. 'Grown-up ones.'

'We don't have them here by choice,' snapped Maggie.

Poppy rolled her eyes. 'Some,' she said. 'There's Mr Minton, still.'

'Your great-uncle?' I asked, working it out as I said it.

Poppy nodded. 'But everyone calls him Mr Minton. And then there's John, though not often.'

'Who's John?' I asked.

'Leon and Minnow's dad,' Poppy said, matter of fact.

Julia nodded. 'My ... person. Boyfriend. Whatever.'

Maggie grunted. And not in a good way.

Julia ignored her. 'He lives in Kalstok mostly though.'

'Where's Kalstok?'

'Just up river,' said Poppy. 'I'll take you there one day.'

One day? How long did she think we were going to be here?

'Where *is* here?' I asked then. Because I know she'd told me No Man's Land, but where was *that*?

'Kernow,' Maggie said. 'Least, the edge of it.'

Kernow. That was on the map. On the very left end of Albion but not part of it, not any more. Independent, like Caledonia, so safe.

Only, why didn't it feel safe?

'Where's *your* dad?' asked Sam then.

Poppy looked at her mum.

'Up country,' said Julia. 'He . . . doesn't believe in what we're doing.'

I felt that insect feeling again. 'What *are* you doing?' I asked.

'The Game,' said Sam. 'Duh.'

'The Game,' said Julia vaguely. 'That's right.'

But the smile had slipped off her face and I knew something wasn't right.

'I expect you'll want a rest,' she said, brightening suddenly. 'Been a long night.'

I shrugged.

'Go on,' she said. 'Go with Maggie and get settled in.'

I didn't understand. 'Aren't we staying with you?'

Julia shook her head. 'Bit full at ours with my three and Leon. Maggie's only got Mr Minton so there's more space.'

Maggie made a sound like a 'humph' and I didn't know if that was good or bad. I was pretty sure it was the second one though. I looked at Poppy like she might have the answer. But how would she? She was only twelve and a girl.

'See you later,' she said.

I shrugged again, like a 'whatever', like I'd do to Paris if it had been her. But soon as I had I felt bad because she wasn't Paris, not even a bit. She wasn't beaky or mean. She was just . . . here.

'Come on then,' snapped Maggie. 'I haven't got all day. And mind you bring your cases.' And off she stomped towards the biggest of the grim buildings.

I could feel my eyes sting then and I had to stop it quick, had to remember what Dad had said: *You've got to be brave ... A hero.*

I picked up my case. 'Come on, Sam,' I said.

Sam slithered off Julia's hip and took his own case in one hand and my hand in the other.

'Come on,' I said again. 'It'll probably be fine.'

But I was talking to me, not Sam.

And I don't think I believed it even then.

TAMAR

'Phone,' said Maggie, soon as we'd got inside.

'What?'

'Not what, pardon,' said Sam.

'Shut up,' I said.

'No, *you* shut up,' said Sam.

'You can both shut up. Now, phone,' Maggie said again. 'Hand it over.'

My hand flapped to the black brick in my pocket. 'Why? It's mine.'

'Because it's not safe.'

'It's just to text my dad. I said I'd be clever.'

'Too clever,' she said then, holding out her hand. 'Or not enough, is my guess.'

I held tight to it. 'But—'

'No buts. That's the rules here. No phones, no

computers, no nothing. Not except under supervision. You can have it back later, and I'll watch you.'

'Watch me?'

'Watch what you're texting.'

'You won't be able to,' I said, sticking my chin out.

'Won't I, indeed?'

'No, you won't,' I said, stubborn as anything, suddenly. 'It'll be in code.'

'Will it now?'

I nodded. Maggie smiled – a half one – but she still held her hand out. And I knew she wouldn't budge so in the end I did it but I felt sick as I did.

'Why's it called Tammer?' Sam asked. 'Is that code?'

Maggie frowned.

'The sign,' said Sam. 'By the door.'

She nodded. 'So you can read then. It's *Tay-mar*, though.'

'Tay-mar,' repeated Sam. 'Tay-maaaar.'

'River,' said a voice from the corner.

I jumped. Sam gasped. We both peered into the gloom.

The voice had come from an old man, older than Maggie and dirty-looking, sat in a chair like a scarecrow. 'Name of the river,' he said again then. 'Tamar. Don't you lot know anything?'

'We're not from here,' I said warily.

'You don't say.'

'Don't mind Mr Minton,' said Maggie. 'He's no worse than me.'

That wasn't saying much.

'I suppose you're foreign, are you?' he said then. 'Black?'

'No,' said Sam. 'Look.' He held out his hands.

The old man raised his eyebrows so I could see the whites of his eyes weren't white at all but yellow, and instead of a black bit in the middle it was milky and dull.

He was blind.

'We're—' I began.

'It doesn't matter what they are,' Maggie snapped at him. 'They're boys, that's all. Only boys.'

'Only boys,' repeated Sam, still showing his hands.

Maggie eyed him. 'Rather have had girls,' she muttered.

Mr Minton snorted.

'Now, go on,' she said, turning to me. 'First up the stairs on the right.'

'I'm not tired,' I said. 'If that's what you think.'

'It's what I know,' she said. 'Go on. I'll wake you when you're needed.'

'Needed?'

'To work,' she said, like it was obvious. 'Or did you think this was a holiday?'

I shook my head. 'I didn't know what it was.'

'It's the Game,' said Sam.

'God help us,' said Maggie, shaking her head. 'God help us.'

But there wasn't a God, not any more. Even Sam knew that. Even most of the Albioneers knew that.

There was just us. People.

Some of us good. And some of us bad.

And it was clearer than ever, I didn't know who was which.

WORK

We did sleep in the end, so Maggie was right about something. It was ten by the time we were up and dressed again. Not that Maggie was happy.

'You'll want wellies,' she said, eyeing Sam's sandals. 'Or your feet'll be filthy.'

'And stamped on,' said Mr Minton.

She didn't correct him, just handed me and Sam an apple each.

'He won't eat it,' I said. 'Not unless it's in a sandwich.'

Mr Minton snorted again.

'Then he'll go hungry,' Maggie snapped. 'Now, boots. Go on.'

'What sort of work is it?' I asked as I wriggled one foot into the red rubber. It was a size too small but Dad hadn't got around to new ones. He hadn't got around to a lot of things lately.

'You'll see,' she said.

***

'It's more like school than work, really,' said Poppy. 'Think of it like that.'

That didn't sound much better and I pulled a face to show so.

'No books though,' she added.

I smiled at that. And it was a real one. Being back with her felt better. Better than being in Tamar anyway.

'What'll we do?'

'Well, you missed the milking.'

'Milking?' My eyes went as wide as the surprise I felt. 'You've got cows?'

'Goats,' Poppy explained. 'And chickens and rabbits.'

'Rabbits!' said Sam. 'Can we milk them?'

Poppy laughed. 'No, but you can help clean them out.'

'I don't mind,' said Sam. 'Rabbit poo is only a two.'

My cheeks went red. 'He's ranked animal poo,'

I explained. 'From ten – that's dog – to one – that's mouse. It's . . . stupid.'

'What about fish?' asked Poppy, as if it wasn't stupid at all.

'Nought,' said Sam. 'Because it gets washed away.'

She nodded. 'Makes sense.'

And all at once I was sad at myself for being embarrassed and angry at Sam for making sense. I wanted to make sense.

'It's because he wanted a pet,' I said. 'But Dad said no because of clearing up poo.'

'Oh, these aren't pets,' Poppy said, frowning.

'What are they then?' asked Sam.

'Are you . . . a farm?' I asked. 'Do you sell things for shops?'

'Sort of,' she said. 'It's more a . . . community.'

'With hardly any men,' Sam said.

Poppy nodded.

'Is all of Kernow like this?' I asked. 'All women and kids?'

Poppy snorted. 'Hardly! Kernow's no better than Albion, not really.'

'But—'

'There's worse than Albioneers, even here. That's what this place is for. A sort of buffer. A place that's . . . neutral. No wars, no fighting. A—'

'A No Man's Land,' I finished, remembering World War One where there'd been a bit of land that wasn't Germany's or ours, just in-between.

Poppy smiled. 'Exactly. Now, come on, or we'll be late. Minnow!' she called out.

A small girl, brown-skinned and pink-booted, with hair that stuck out in every direction, came out of the house.

'This is my sister,' said Poppy.

'I was six last week,' she said.

'I'll be six soon,' said Sam, like he'd scored a goal. 'December twenty-ninth. Almost Christmas. Almost like Jesus.'

I don't know why he added that. We didn't believe in Jesus. And I could tell no one here did either.

'And this is her brother, Leon.' Poppy nodded to a tall boy in the doorway, brown as well, browner than Minnow. He didn't say anything.

Just stared. Not as bad as Mr Minton but different all the same.

'Is he all right?' I said, quietly as I could.

Poppy laughed. 'Fine as you and me,' she said. 'Maybe better.'

I felt my cheeks redden again. 'What about Noah?'

'He's in the woods fetching kindling,' said Poppy, like she was glad of it. 'You'll probably see him later though.'

Kindling. I didn't know what it was but I didn't want to ask and look stupid. Not again.

'Wood,' she said, as if she could see right in me.

I bristled. 'I knew that.'

'OK.'

'I did,' I insisted.

Paris would have argued. Would have said I was a liar liar pants on fire. Even Ahmed would have called me out. But Poppy didn't. She just shrugged and smiled and walked into the shimmer of sunshine.

And I followed her. We all did. Me and Minnow

and Leon and Sam, all heading across the yard to where Julia was already bent over a bucket with a brush in her hand.

RABBITS

The rabbit shed was at the end of the low building, just down from the goats. They had a run as well, and the goats had a field in the daytime. The chickens had a coop and a yard, and a fence that stretched over the lot because of foxes.

'Here.' Julia handed me a sort of spade. 'This is for scooping. Dump it in the bucket and then you put clean straw in. OK?'

I nodded. 'What do you do with it? The poo, I mean. Do you put it in bags?'

Poppy made a noise like a cough and I knew I'd messed up again.

'We grow stuff with it, silly,' said Minnow.

'Or burn it once it's dried,' added Julia. 'Waste not, want not.'

Something in me jumped. Mum had said that! When I was too full for the last bit of fish finger and she'd pop it in her mouth and say, 'Waste not, want not'.

But I couldn't say that. Not here, not now. Just stored it in my mind for later, for the list. 'Why's Maggie not working?' I asked instead, and scooped another handful of wet straw into the bucket. 'Is she too old?'

Julia laughed, her mouth wide so I could see her teeth whiter than white. 'Oh, it's all all right,' she said quick. 'I'm not laughing at you.'

'I know,' I said, shifting on my feet. Then I realised what I was doing – shifting was code for being worried – and stopped.

'No one's too old,' she said. 'She just . . . does a different job.'

'Like Noah?'

She paused. 'Sort of.'

'Is he . . . chopping down wood?' I wanted to know. Wanted to know what he was doing and why I couldn't do it too.

'Christ, no,' said Julia, picking up a rabbit – all grey and mottled, not white like the ones at the zoo – and moving it out of the way. 'Noah and axes don't mix at the best of times. Just twigs he's after.'

So kindling *was* wood, but small bits.

'Would it be better if we were girls?' I said then.

'What?'

'Maggie said. She said she wanted girls.'

'Oh, love. You've got to understand. It's not you. But men . . . men took her partner.'

'Like her husband?'

'Wife,' said Julia. 'Laura, she was called' – she corrected herself – '*is* called.'

So Maggie was a lesbian. Ms Kitteridge from number seventeen was a lesbian. She was one of the first to go. Mr Metcalfe saw to that.

'Where is she now? Laura, I mean.'

'We don't know, love. Maggie's working on it.'

Sadness swelled in me like a balloon. 'Why'd she have us at all if she doesn't like boys— I mean, men.'

'Because there's a war coming,' said Julia. 'And that's what good people do.'

NOAH

We ate lunch in the yard – Poppy on the grass, and me and Sam and Minnow and Leon sitting on the wall.

Leon didn't say much, but he watched everything, saw everything. I could tell he was storing things in his head. Like I do sometimes. Not for ammo, like Jayden Nesbitt, but for interest. I know because he remembered our names, and exactly how old Sam was. 'Five years, six months, seventeen days,' he said, nodding at Sam.

'When's your birthday?' Poppy asked me.

'Next month,' I said, hesitant. 'August the second.'

'We can have a party!' Poppy said.

'With the rabbits!' added Sam.

My stomach shifted. 'We won't be here by then,' I said. 'But thanks.'

'Ten years, eleven months, fourteen days,' Leon said then.

Poppy grinned. 'Told you.'

Lunch was sandwiches so I didn't have to say anything about Sam. Julia had made them. Though I wasn't sure what was in them. A kind of meat and pickle, only not Branston like at home but something green and gloopy and home-made. Sam scraped his off and dropped it on the grass. Only, Leon scooped it up again on a finger and licked it off. Then he laughed. 'Lush,' he said.

So Sam did it again, dropped the pickle, and watched Leon pick it up and lick it. Then Minnow was at it too. And then Leon held some out to Minnow and she licked it off Leon's finger. Then he did the same to Sam and Sam actually swallowed it, not even in a sandwich, and he's never done that, not even chocolate, not even for Dad.

'Freaks,' said someone.

I jumped and turned.

A boy was standing there, tall as a stalk and thin and all. Hair blond as Poppy's but shaved short and stubbly like the fur on a toy rabbit. And I knew who he was without asking.

Noah.

'There's more in the kitchen,' said Poppy. 'If you're hungry.'

He pulled a face. 'I'll make my own.' His eyes fixed on me then, beady and keen. 'Who's that?'

'Alan,' said Poppy before I could open my mouth.

''Nother one of *them*?' he said, nodding at Leon.

'No,' I said quick. I didn't know what 'them' meant but I knew Noah didn't like it. 'And that's Sam,' I said. 'My brother.'

'It's started then,' Noah said to Poppy.

Poppy shrugged and I wanted to know what had started but Sam got in first.

'We cleaned rabbits,' he said. 'Mine's called Dave.'

Noah snorted, but not in a happy way. 'They're not pets,' he said, same as Poppy, but thinner, sharper.

'What are they then?' I asked.

'Dinner.' He grinned.

I stopped chewing, a wodge of cold meat lodged in my mouth.

'Ignore him,' said Poppy. 'It's pork. John traded.'

I knew what traded meant, and that it wasn't a lie, but I swallowed hard to get rid anyway.

Noah shrugged and I saw the muscles in his arms, tight as a Marvel man. 'You can't call one Dave anyway. Dave's not a rabbit's name.'

'Is too,' said Sam, all sing-song.

'Is not.'

'Is too!'

'Shut up.' Noah kicked at the grit and a puff of dust went up.

'Leave him alone,' I said. 'He's only five.'

'And six months,' added Sam.

'And seventeen days.'

'Shut up.' Noah rounded on Leon. Then scuffed at the dirt again. 'Like I care.'

I could feel anger in me then, bubbling up. And even though I didn't have muscles like Noah or anyone from Marvel or DC, I knew this was how Hulk felt when he was going to change. 'We'll be gone soon,' I spat at him. 'So you won't have to care at all.'

But Noah just raised one eyebrow and smirked. 'That what you reckon?'

I looked at Poppy to back me up but she just shrugged and the anger fizzled out into something else cold and shivery. I stood up.

'Where do you think you're going?' laughed Noah. 'Home?'

'Maggie's,' I snapped. 'I need to do something.'

'She's out,' said Poppy. 'Won't be back for hours.'

'So I'll wait.'

'You'll miss weaving,' she said. 'I could show you how to make nettle thread.'

'Like I care,' I said, parroting Noah.

And right then I almost meant it.

DINNER

I didn't wait in the kitchen, because Mr Minton was there, all yellow and leathery. I sat on the front step in the shade and watched the others with the nettles, Poppy grasping them as if they were nothing, not stingers at all, cutting off the leaves, then stripping the innards out to dry before slowly winding the green into strands like magic. Always careful not to let Minnow or Sam touch until it was safe.

And I wanted to try, I did. But I wasn't giving in to Noah, no way. Wherever he was. Whoever he was.

Who was he? I mean, I knew he was Poppy's brother, and Minnow's half one, but he wasn't like either of them. Or like his mum. They were all light and laughs and he was dark and glowering anger. And I wondered then about his dad up country, and why he'd gone and what he was doing now. I could've asked Poppy, I suppose. But I was too cross still. And besides, I had my own dad to think about. Wondering what he was up to right now, without us. Not weaving nettles or mucking about with rabbits that's for sure. And I wondered as well why he'd sent us, if he knew enough about No Man's Land. Knew it was nearly all women and animals. No school. No telly. No nothing.

No wonder Noah was angry.

***

It was nearly four when Maggie got back.

'Welcoming committee, is it?' she said, bustling past me.

'No,' I said, following her in. 'I just need to text my dad.'

'Can't it wait?' She dumped a bag on the table.

'No!' I said, loud. Too loud. Then again, softer, 'No. It's . . . important.'

She looked at me like she was trying to see in me, what I was up to. 'All right,' she said eventually. 'Wait there.'

'I can get it,' I said.

She laughed. 'Do you think I'm stupid?'

'No, I . . .'

'Good.'

She stamped into the back and I snatched a look at Mr Minton, who was snickering.

'You'll not get the better of her,' he said. 'No one can.'

'I wasn't . . .' I began, but I couldn't say it. Another lie. Because I knew he'd see through me, even with his broken eyes. Instead I just stared at the calendar on the wall and counted the seconds until Maggie was back.

'Here,' she said.

Thirty-seven. Enough to get to the end of the corridor. To the 'pantry', she'd called it.

'Thanks,' I mumbled.

'Go on then,' she said, waiting.

'I'm thinking,' I replied.

Because I couldn't just say what I meant, could I? Couldn't just blurt out, 'I hate it here come and get me everyone's awful.' I had to be clever, like Dad had told me.

Then I remembered something Dad had shown me. An old code – not like the kind he cracked at Albion Interception, but from before then, before World War One. Before Henry the Eighth even.

A Caesar shift, it was called, after the Roman emperor. All you had to do was move the letters of the alphabet along so e.g. A became B and B became C. And it took me a minute 'cause I had to do it in my head, couldn't ask for scrap paper even. But in the end I got it.

J XBOU UP DONF IPNF I wrote.

I WANT TO COME HOME

'What's that?' asked Maggie peering at it.

'Code,' I said. 'You wouldn't understand.'

'No,' she replied. 'Too old and stupid for that. Just a woman.'

Mr Minton snickered again and I felt bad. But not that bad. She was the one beaking after all.

The text came back in a minute.

2 BVHVTU, it said. 2 AUGUST. And my insides fizzed and Noah and Maggie could go do one.

'Good news?' asked Maggie.

I nodded. 'Can I add something? On the calendar I mean?'

Maggie stared for a second, then handed me a red felt pen. 'Go on.'

I put a ring round August 2nd.

'What's that?'

'Nothing. My birthday, that's all.'

But it wasn't just that. It was D-Day. The day Dad was coming to fetch us. So I added a D in the middle and all. There was another ring, I saw then. Round the 9th. 'What's that?' I asked.

Maggie looked. Then took the pen back off me. 'Nothing,' she said. 'Just something I need to remember, that's all.

'A birthday?'

She shook her head. 'Now go on.'

'Go where?' I asked.

'I don't care. I've got dinner to make.'

'What's for dinner?'

'Stew,' she said.

I felt my stomach slide. 'Rabbit?'

She laughed. 'That Noah been at you, has he?

No, it's vegetable. Not that it's up to you.'

The relief was sweet. 'Can you put it in a sandwich?' I asked. 'Just for Sam?'

Maggie pulled a face. 'I'll do no such thing,' she said. 'Now, scram.'

***

She didn't do any such thing. But she'd left two bits of bread on the side – brown and seedy, but beggars couldn't be choosers, I supposed, and so I dolloped the stew on one slice of bread and popped the other slice on top for him.

Sam peered at it like it might be poison but he ate it anyway.

'Hungry work, farm work,' Mr Minton said, like he could tell Sam was gulping it down.

'Can . . . can you see him?' I asked.

'Smell him, more like,' said Mr Minton, and cackled, as if he was a witch not a man.

'I did do a fart,' admitted Sam.

I felt my face heat up.

But Maggie shrugged. 'Everyone does it.' And then, she shifted on her chair like she was lifting a bum cheek, and let out a sound like a machine gun.

Sam roared. So did Mr Minton. Even Ahmed would've been proud of that one.

I just sat there with my eyes wide and my fingers holding my nose.

'How come poo knows not to come out?' asked Sam. 'When you fart.'

'Just does,' said Maggie.

'So, it's like a decision you make with your bum?' Sam checked.

Maggie smiled. Smiled! 'I suppose it is,' she said.

'Are you deciding now?' asked Sam.

Maggie smiled again. And then she let out another little one as if to prove it. 'Decision made.'

And then I was more confused than ever. Because Maggie didn't even want boys but now here she was doing farts to order for Sam. And so maybe she was all right after all. Not a hero but not a villain either.

Just an ordinary person. Like us.

***

She still sent us to bed at seven though.

'Seven's for babies, everyone knows that,' said Sam. But he was half-asleep already, could hardly lift his drink.

'You'll get used to it,' she said after me as we headed for the stairs.

I stopped and turned. 'Used to what?'

'The country.'

I shrugged. 'Maybe,' I said, and turned and trudged up to bed.

But I wouldn't. I didn't have to. 'Cause in two weeks Dad would be here. And then everything would be back to how it was supposed to be.

Everything would be back to normal.

NORMAL
(twelve days until D-Day)

There was nothing normal about No Man's Land. Not Mr Minton with his milky eyes. Not the weird milk we had on cereal. Not the fact that the cereal wasn't even cereal it was just oats and seeds and something called dates, which felt like eating a beetle.

Sam ate it though.

'What about a sandwich?' I said. 'Don't you want it in bread?'

'Don't be silly,' he said. 'The milk would drip.'

Maggie made another sort of harumph noise at that, which I'd learnt meant she was happy. Though mostly it was hard to tell; she'd not smiled since the farting thing, and most of the time she wasn't even around. I'd learnt she went to talk to other women. That's what Poppy said. To spread the word.

'About what?'

'About living like this,' Poppy said. 'In a . . . neutral community.'

'Are there others then?'

'Other communities?'

I nodded.

'One or two,' Poppy said. 'But we were the first, I think. Least in Kernow.'

I'd learnt loads from Poppy, matter of fact.

I'd learnt that she hadn't been to school since she was eight, and Julia pulled her and Noah out, said there was enough to learn at home.

I'd learnt that Noah was none too happy about that, even though he hated school. Said it made him look like a right weirdo, and his dad would never have let it happen if he was there, only he wasn't.

I'd learnt he'd tried to run away once, got as far as Kalstok before John brought him back kicking and screaming and saying he'd rather die in Albion than live in No Man's Land, only John said he wouldn't say that if he knew the truth about Albion. But John didn't say what the truth was, because I checked and Poppy didn't know.

I'd learnt where the weird milk came from and all.

Goats.

Three of them – Shirley and Mabel and Mo, white-faced and lop-eared with eyes like snakes but smiling in spite of it. We had to milk them every morning, me and Poppy and Julia. Just us. Leon didn't like them, and Minnow and Sam were too small not to get kicked, Poppy said, so they had to do the rabbits or sit with Mr Minton. I wondered then if Mr Minton knew Minnow was half-black, and Leon totally black, and decided he definitely didn't or he'd be more like Mr Metcalfe about it and probably report them.

'Won't *we* get kicked?' I said, not fancying that or getting close to them at all with their strange smell and their bleating like a baby's cry.

Perhaps Mr Minton would be better, after all.

Poppy shook her head. 'Not if you're nice to them.'

I pulled a face.

'Come on,' Julia said. 'Here.'

And she sat me down on a little stool, and crouched behind me. 'Take the teat,' she said. 'But softly.'

The teat was the nipple, I knew that. But not like a human one. This one was spotted and long and dangly. 'I can't,' I said.

'Yes, you can,' said Julia. And she took my hand in hers and closed both around it.

It was warmer than I'd thought, and not as weird. But weird enough. I mean, what was Ahmed doing right now? Asleep probably. Or playing *Doom*. No one else had to hold goat boobs before breakfast, I knew that much. Not even Noah.

'Now squeeze,' she said. 'Gentle, though.'

I gritted my teeth and squeezed.

Nothing happened.

'It's OK,' said Julia. 'Let's do it together.'

This time the squeeze started at the top with my big finger and worked its way down to my little one and with it came a long jet of hot milk, straight into the tin.

'Oh my God!' I said.

'There you go. Not so bad, is it?'

I shook my head. It wasn't.

'Now you try.'

So I did. I tried – both hands this time, because of there being two teats – and it took a few goes but then I managed it and I even got into the rhythm, until the tin was half-full and the goat was empty, with only thin drips coming out.

'Good girl, Shirley,' said Julia, patting the goat's neck. 'See?'

I did see. And I patted Shirley as well. 'How'd you learn it?' I asked then. 'Was it at university?'

Julia laughed. 'No, love. I grew up here, remember? My mum – Maggie's sister – only moved away after I'd left for uni. That's where I met your mum. She'd grown up in London, mind.'

'You mean Londinium?'

Julia pulled a face. 'If you say so.'

I nodded then, remembering Horrible Nan

and her house there, all grim and stingy, like her. So I thought of something else.

'Why've they got names?' I asked. 'The goats, I mean.'

'Because we don't eat them,' said Julia.

'But you do eat the rabbits?'

She nodded, solemn. 'We have to,' she said.

'Why?' I asked.

Poppy shrugged. 'Because that's how it is now.'

DAVE
(ten days until D-Day)

But it wasn't. Least not quite. Because when me and Poppy got to the rabbit hutches one morning, Sam and Minnow had named all of them.

'This one's Dave, this one's Harry Potter and this one's Hermione.' Sam pointed at three of them in turn.

I frowned. 'How can you even tell the difference?'

'Leon can.'

I looked at Leon. He looked back.

'But how?' I asked him.

'Because he's a weirdo.'

My stomach jumped. Noah was back.

'What are you up to?' he said, straight at me.

'I . . . They've named them,' I said.

'Alan?' Poppy had her hands up, like I was an eejit.

Perhaps I was. I looked at her, then at Noah, then at her again. 'It just . . . it came out.' It had. I hadn't meant to but something about him made me say it.

'Mum'll go mad,' he said.

'Can't you just keep these ones?' I asked, desperate then.

'And then what'll we eat?' He stuck his hands on his hips, chest out, head to one side, waiting.

'I don't know? Can't you just go to the shops and get meat from there? In packets?'

Noah snorted. 'What shops? It's ten miles to the nearest town and when you get there do you know how expensive it is?'

I remembered Dad cooking then: how we'd stopped having burgers every Friday. And then bacon on a Saturday. And then the ham in our sandwiches turned into spread.

'Anyway, those animals lead terrible lives,' said Poppy.

'But . . . what does it matter if they all end up dead?' I said.

Poppy glared at me. 'Do you really believe that?'

'I don't . . . I don't know?'

'Why are *we* bothering then?' Poppy shot at me. 'We're all going to end up dead as well.'

Sam yelped at that.

'Not now,' said Poppy, turning to him quick. 'Just . . . one day.'

'Sooner if you don't wise up,' said Noah.

'Shut up,' she snapped at him. Then turned back to me. 'Anyway, that's not the point. The point is, would you be happy spending the rest of your life locked up like a criminal?'

I thought of Maggie's Laura and felt sick with shame. 'I'm sorry,' I said.

'Don't be,' said Noah. 'You don't have to apologise to her.' He nodded at me.

I didn't know who to look at, or who to side with. Or even what the sides were.

Poppy sighed. 'Just think about it,' she said.

***

I did think about it. But all I could think was that death was everywhere here. And that Dad had got it all wrong.

J EPH'U MJLF JU IFSF I wrote when I texted him that night.

'Very mysterious,' said Maggie as she took back the phone.

'Good,' I said. 'It's meant to be.'

But when the reply came, all it said was **US2**. TRY.

THE WOMEN
(seven days until D-Day)

The least normal thing about No Man's Land was the women.

Not just Julia and Maggie – and Poppy and Minnow, if you counted the girls – but the others that came and went at all hours. No chaperones, no one to check on them. Just women being bold and mouthy. Like 'dogs off their leads', as Mr Metcalfe used to say.

Or like men.

They came and sat in the kitchen at Maggie's, smoking old-fashioned cigarettes that they rolled themselves, like in films, and saying swears and laughing about stuff I didn't understand and whispering about stuff I couldn't hear even though

I tried with a glass against the wall, like Dad had showed us so we could listen in to the Metcalfes for a laugh. Only, Mr Metcalfe was shouting at Mrs Metcalfe and then there was a bang and no one was laughing after that. Not for a long time.

It wasn't that I didn't like women. I really did. Julia and Poppy, and Maggie at times. And back home, Mrs King was brilliant. Even Paris had her moments. But so many of them together felt dangerous – like a powder keg waiting to blow. Albion had stopped it, all the women gathering together. They must've done that for a reason. Mustn't they?

Dad can't have realised what he'd got us into. Because what if the army came? What if they got caught? Then we'd all be for it.

I said it to Poppy, asked her how she dared, how they all dared; weren't they worried about being arrested?

But she just laughed. 'Don't be soft,' she said. 'This is No Man's Land.'

Like that was the answer to everything.

But I missed men. I missed Ahmed with his games and his ideas and his plans to conquer the world. I missed Dad's mate Ringo, who could throw a boomerang and drink a pint of milk in one go.

But most of all I missed Dad. I missed him calling me 'clever kid' and 'mate' like I was one. I missed him flipping fish fingers and singing to the music on his phone. And I missed him kissing me goodnight, and saying 'see you later, alligator' even though sometimes he was gone before we even got up. The only men here were Mr Minton who couldn't see and Leon who couldn't do much except maths and rabbits and Noah who couldn't care less about anyone, or so he said. John came and went but mostly went. Because of Maggie, I think. But also because he had to work – though at what I wasn't sure and Poppy wasn't clear.

Poppy said it shouldn't matter, and that I could be friends with girls just as much as boys. 'That's how it was,' she said. 'In the before days. That's why we have boys here.'

'Just not men,' I said.

'Not yet,' she said.

I didn't ask about that because that was the future, and what did that matter? We'd be gone by then. What mattered was now, and why Noah didn't want to know me, even though we were the only boys here, apart from Sam and Leon.

I thought about it a lot.

When we were milking in the mornings.

When we were sat down for dinner and I'd see Noah skulk across the yard and slip into the kitchen at Julia's, then out again soon as he'd eaten.

When me and Sam were playing cards in Maggie's kitchen with Leon, and Leon won and Maggie clapped him on the back like he was her very own grandson, and Mr Minton said he was a right little 'card sharp' only Sam thought he said 'shark' and sang 'Baby Shark' for the rest of the game even though Mr Minton begged him to stop. And I wished Noah was there because I thought he might like it, actually, hanging out with the boys. Even if one of them was practically a hundred and smelt of cough medicine, and one of them was Leon, and one was me.

Maybe it's just because he just doesn't know me, I thought. Maybe I could be his 'mate' if he only gave me the chance.

And so one morning, after milking, I set off to find him.

***

He wasn't in his room, which is where Poppy said he spent most of his time. Or in the woods, working. I had to search the whole farm – in the stables, and even the old coal store, which was where they kept the sacks from trading, which meant swapping food with other people – potatoes, mostly, or apples when they had them.

It was in the folly I found him. The folly was a turret on the path watching over the river. Round and grey and glinting. Built for nothing but fun, in the olden days when they could afford stuff like that. Could afford fun. Least that's what Mrs King had told us.

I pushed open the wooden door, and saw him squatting on the floor with a piece of wood and a knife. My heart was fast as a mouse but I spoke all the same.

'What are you doing?' I asked.

'What's it to you?' He didn't even look up. Just carried on scraping at the branch with the blade.

'I've got a penknife,' I said. 'It's got eleven gadgets on it, even scissors.'

He flicked his eyes up at me for a second, then back to his work. 'I suppose you think that makes you special?'

'No,' I said quickly. 'Just . . .' – I snatched at something – 'you can borrow it if you want.'

Noah stopped and stared. 'Maybe,' he said.

And I felt like I'd been given a tick, some golden time, like Mrs King used to hand out if we got questions right or didn't fight.

'You got a phone?' he said then.

I nodded.

'Can I borrow it?'

'Haven't you got your own?'

He shook his head. 'Stupid woman took it. Yonks ago.'

He meant Julia, I knew it. And I knew she wasn't stupid and all. And that he shouldn't say that about her, not his own mum. But I had to nod, didn't I?

Not that it made any difference. 'I don't have it though,' I said. 'Maggie took it.' Then, I took a breath. 'Stupid woman,' I added. And I felt a weird shimmer in me when I did it: a buzzy feeling. But not a good one.

Noah liked it though. Smiled. Quick and neat. 'But you could find it?'

I felt the shimmer in me again, but covered it with a shrug. 'I don't know. Maybe?'

Maybe I could. I hadn't tried, after all.

Noah nodded. Then he pulled up his right trouser leg, and under the little hairs was a stamp of black ink in the shape of a sword.

A tattoo.

'I can do you one of these,' he said.

I felt a tremor in my legs. 'How?' I managed.

He held up his blade.

'Maybe,' I said again. 'Only, I don't think my school would like it. Or my dad,' I added.

He snorted. 'You actually think you're going home?'

I nodded. I was going home. Soon. Wasn't I?

Noah shook his head. 'Maybe you *are* as dumb as a girl,' he said.

'I'm not,' I insisted, even though most of the girls I knew were cleverer than me. Poppy definitely was.

He stared for a second, sizing me up like Maggie had done. 'We'll see,' he said. 'Find the phone and I might change my mind, mate.'

'Mate', he'd said!

'OK,' I promised.

So I had to, didn't I?

A promise to a mate was a promise, after all. Even in No Man's Land.

LAST ON THE LEFT
(six days until D-Day)

I waited until the afternoon – after the goats and the rabbits and the lunch on the wall. And after Maggie had gone wherever it was she went to. Then I told Poppy I needed the loo, I'd only be a minute, and I crept back in, not through the kitchen, where Mr Minton lurked, sweaty and fretting to himself, but in the front door, and straight down to the pantry at the back.

She always came down this corridor when I'd asked to text before. Always taken the same number of seconds. So the phone had to be hidden somewhere round here. Probably in with the pickles and things – jars and jars of them. All labelled with dates: beetroot and onions and eggs. Dad's mate Ringo once ate ten pickled eggs in a row and then farted so hard he said he'd had to change his pants. I promised myself I wasn't going to eat even one of them – not that I'd need to. Not with Dad coming soon.

But the phone wasn't behind the eggs anyway.

And it wasn't in the little wire cupboard with the cheese, or in the drawers with the spices or even in the fridge.

I slammed the door in anger and leant back on it, and that's when I saw it. Not the phone, something else. Something that made my whole body wobble and I thought I'd have to change my pants there and then.

It was a gun.

Not a small, shining one, like in films. This one was long and mottled and from the olden days. But a gun all the same. Just sitting there, wedged between the washing machine and the ironing board. But why was it here? Didn't only baddies have guns? In real life anyway. Did that mean Maggie was a villain after all?

I reached out a hand to touch it when the door

behind me creaked and I whirled round, my cheeks burning and my stomach tight.

Poppy!' I blurted.

'What are you doing?' she said.

'Nothing, I . . .' But I couldn't lie and I couldn't tell the truth either. So I just shifted slightly, so she wouldn't see what I'd seen. 'I was just nosing,' I said.

'You want to watch it,' she replied, serious as anything. 'No secrets around here. Even the walls have ears!'

And that snapped in me – and I remembered then. Mum said that – number 13! I couldn't remember why or when but she'd said it to Dad once and I'd looked for them – the ears – but I didn't know then it was code for 'anyone could be listening'.

Poppy was joking, that was all. And I made myself laugh even though I wasn't happy.

Poppy smiled back. 'John called. You want to come to Kalstok tomorrow?'

'Kalstok?'

'I said, remember? Up river?'

I nodded. 'If you like.'

'Oh, well, if you're not bothered.'

'No, I do!' I blurted. Noah wouldn't mind, would he? I didn't have to enjoy it, after all. Hanging around with a girl.

And if he was annoyed, well, I might not have the phone, but I had something, didn't I? Something better.

I had a gun.

***

I still wanted the phone though. If not for Noah then for me. But I had to be clever about it. I needed more clues. So after dinner I asked Maggie if I could text, then when she was out of the room I followed her.

'She's not stupid,' said Mr Minton.

I stopped, swung round.

'Nor am I,' he carried on. 'Ears like a bat. Only good thing about losing your eyes.'

'I . . . I wasn't doing anything,' I said.

'A likely story.'

My cheeks were red with shame. But he couldn't see them, could he? Any more than he could know where the phone was or why I was after it.

So I peered, just long enough to see Maggie come out of a door at the end of the corridor then shut it behind her.

Last door on the left, I said to myself. *Not the pantry – the study!*

Back in the kitchen Maggie handed me the phone, hovering as I typed.

IYSSZ YQ I said. HURRY UP.

OPU ZFU came the text back.

I felt sick. NOT YET, he'd replied.

Then I thought about that word: 'yet'. 'Yet' wasn't a no, was it? It was a time. 'Yet' meant he was definitely coming. Not tomorrow. But soon.

On the second of August.

'Here,' said Maggie. 'I'll have that, thank you.'

I held the phone out and she glanced at it. Then back at me.

'Not long,' she said. 'Tuesday.'

And I should have got it then.

But it wasn't for days that I knew what she'd done.

THE BRIDGE
(five days until D-Day)

We went there by river – me and Poppy. Minnow and Sam wanted to come but Julia said Sam was too small to be out with us, seeing as he couldn't swim. I could though – a hundred metres front crawl and breast stroke; I'd got certificates. Not that I was going to need certificates or even my trunks. Not in that water. Because we had a boat.

Kitty, she was called. All boats have names, Poppy explained, and they're all 'she' as well. When I asked her why though she just shrugged and pulled hard on the oars again, the brown sack between her feet, ready for trading.

I hadn't asked but I knew what was in it. Dead things.

'You don't like men much,' I said.

'They're all right,' she said. 'But it's men that got us into this mess and it'll be women that get us out. That's what Maggie says.'

I felt ashamed then. Of who I was, even though Albion wasn't my idea, or Dad's or Ringo's or any of our friends'.

'Anyway, I like you,' she said.

I went hot with that and flustered. 'And Sam,' I blurted.

She nodded. 'And Leon and even Noah when he's not in a mood. It's just . . . there's a lot that's rotten.'

I thought about everything she'd said. 'There are Albioneers even here then? In No Man's Land I mean?'

Poppy nodded. 'Though they won't admit it.'

I thought of Mr Minton then, sour and scowling with his 'Johnny foreigners' and his 'not like us' comments. Only, he liked Leon and Minnow well enough. Because how can you tell what anyone looks like when your eyes don't work? More truth that way maybe, I realised. Unless you're already too rotten to hear it.

But it wasn't just men anyway. Women went along with it and all – with Albion. Mrs Metcalfe, Paris, Horrible Nan. And I wondered then if Maggie was one of them. A secret Albioneer. If that's what she was up to when she went missing for hours, or was shut in her study. Maybe all the men-hating was a pretence. Maybe all this was a pretence.

She was a Minton, after all. And she had a gun.

And what about Julia? She was a sort of a Minton and all.

I felt sick soon as I'd thought that one though. She couldn't be bad. She'd been a friend of Mum's. And she was kind and clever and careful with me and Sam. Like that morning, she'd slapped sun cream on me even though I'd said I was all right, thanks. But then I was glad of it. Round the farm was different – there it was all damp and brackeny. But out on the water I was right under the sun, and I could feel my skin pinking, see Poppy's turn from milk to biscuit, see the hairs on our arms glistening. I could tell then it was almost August.

Almost time.

But I couldn't think about Dad right then because that was when I saw it – Kalstok. Only, not just the village – the houses all hugger-mugger on the hill, the boatyard below, the church with the black-and-white flag on top (Kernow's flag, Poppy told me) – but above it all, spreadeagled across the valley, the biggest bridge I'd ever seen.

It was so tall it made me squint and feel dizzy – ten arches, higher than the hills, as if it was nudging the sun itself. It was incredible, but menacing too. As if it wasn't dead exactly, but pretending.

'It's the viaduct,' said Poppy.

'What's a viaduct?'

'A bridge for trains.'

'There are trains?'

Poppy shook her head. 'Not any more. The station got shut along with the border. Too dangerous. Now you've got to get down to Essa on this side, almost to Plym Mouth on that. Not that we're allowed.'

'Plym Mouth?' I said, remembering Dad's map.

'But that's . . .' I looked across at the right bank of the river, all reedy. At the woods rising up behind. That was Albion, right there, all along. And Dad somewhere in it.

And at once I could see him, hear him, smell him even: sweaty from driving or bleary from sleep. And I wanted him more than ever then.

'Didn't you realise?' Poppy asked. 'The river – that's sort of the border. No one owns it, so they can't keep us off there, but we're not supposed to dock on the other side. Fetching you, well, that was a risk.'

No one owns it. No Man's Land.

I hadn't got it at all.

'Earth to Alan,' Poppy said then.

'Huh?' I asked, coming to.

'I said "come on".' She pulled the oars into the boat and then grabbed on to a post along the bank, hauling the boat up so she could hook over a rope. 'We're here.'

KALSTOK

The village didn't look like a trading post. It didn't look like anything at all; the shops and pubs as dead as the viaduct. In one window, the corpses of fat flies lay on their backs alongside cracked china and flopped-over dolls. In another, a sign lay on its side, asking for motorbikes 'dead or alive', which I knew was code for working or not working and I wondered what for.

'It wasn't always like this,' Poppy told me as we walked along a back street, narrow as a passage and just as dim. 'Once, tourists came, and before that there was industry.'

'What industry?'

'Mines and stuff, I think. Albion was supposed to bring everything back, wasn't it. But we got nothing.

No one did.'

But there must be jobs. There had to be. That's what Mr Metcalfe was always saying. 'Jobs for Albion, jobs for all!' That's what they fought for. Although Ahmed's uncle had been sacked and his sister was still looking for work a year after leaving school.

'So now what do people do?' I asked. 'For money, I mean.'

'This,' she held up the sack. 'We trade.'

***

I don't know what Poppy gave John or John gave Poppy but she seemed happy enough with it – whatever it was we had in the bag now. And John was happy too – hugging Poppy like she was his own. She hugged him back and all.

'Why doesn't he live at the farm?' I asked. 'If he's Minnow and Leon's dad and – you know – your mum's . . .'

'Boyfriend?'

I nodded.

'It's just . . . better this way. For now.'

'But why? Mr Minton can't see him,' I said. 'He wouldn't know.'

Poppy snorted. 'You think that's why? Because he's black?'

I shrugged. 'I don't know. Is it Maggie then?'

Poppy shook her head. 'It's just . . . his job. It's easier if he's out here. Nearer—'

She stopped herself but I knew what she was going to say. Nearer Albion.

'What does he even do?'

'Stuff,' she said eventually, dumping the sack in the boat with a thud. 'None of your business.'

I felt bad then but angry too, a flicker of it, hot and bothering in me. Why wasn't I allowed to know anything? No TV at home, no nothing here and no one telling me why or what for.

'I'm not a kid,' I said then. 'I start secondary in September.'

She looked at me then, her face strange. Maybe she was sorry, but if she was, she didn't say so.

Instead she said. 'Go on then. If you're so big, you can row.'

***

Rowing wasn't as easy as I'd thought though. However hard I pulled, nothing glided, nothing swooshed, it flapped and splashed and almost sunk at one point, an oar dropped in the water and one swinging round so it practically thwacked Poppy.

'You'll get the hang of it,' she said, rescuing both. 'Eventually.'

Eventually. I was going home in five days and rowing would take longer than that for the knack.

'Here.' She gestured at me to swap places, and sweaty and sulking I slumped in the back of the boat.

'I've got a better idea anyway,' she said.

I peered at her from under my damp, lanky fringe. 'What?' I said, as if I didn't care either way.

'You'll see,' she said.

'Whatever,' I said.

But it wasn't whatever. Just like I knew it wouldn't be.

Because nothing in No Man's Land ever was.

SWIMMING

'I'm not swimming in that,' I said.

We were standing on the beach – if you can call it that. Just a thick sludge of mud from the edge of the woods to the water, really. But the water was worse – a murky blur of brown and green. Like soup. With flies on.

'It's clean,' Poppy insisted.

That's what Dad had said about the pool round the corner but even that had hair in it and plasters and once, a poo. And that water smelt of clean. This smelt of outside.

'I haven't got my trunks,' I said, like that would put an end to it.

'I haven't got my costume,' Poppy replied. And then, not even hiding herself, she pulled off her dress and stood there, in knickers and a bra thing. I tried to imagine Paris Metcalfe doing that. Or any of the girls in our class. They'd sooner die. 'Up to you,' she said then. 'But I'm going in.'

And I watched as she waded out and then, quick as a fish, dived under, rising again with her hair drenched and her skin glistening. 'Come on!' she called. Then she held her nose and ducked under again, before springing up downriver.

And she looked free and it looked easy and somehow before I knew what I was doing I was down to my pants and picking my way into the sinking silt.

It was cold, colder than I'd reckoned, especially when it got to my bits, and I gasped at the shock of it.

'Jump under,' Poppy told me. 'It's the only way.'

So I held my breath and counted – one, two, THREE! – and then I was in and – oh! – the feel of it, like swimming in thick silk, not like the pool or the lido at all. And under the water were fish,

I knew it, silvery millions of them skittering around my feet, while above me tiny white-bellied birds barrelled low across the water, black arrows across the green.

'Swifts,' said Poppy, nodding at them. 'Only here for the summer.'

Like me, I thought then, and for an instant I felt sad – for the birds and me – because this was the life, wasn't it? Swimming in rivers?

Then I heard it – a 'yeehaw!' that scattered the flapping and came with a crash into the water that sent arcs of it soaring up with the birds.

'Leon!' complained Poppy. But she was smiling really. And I saw why.

Leon surfaced, silver trickles of water rolling off him like he was oilskin, his shoulders wide, his ribs skinny. Then he hollered again – a wild, free sound – and dived, sliding through the inky water like he was an eel, grabbing my legs, so I yelped as well.

And then we were all at it – all three of us – whooping and hollering and sending out waves.

And right then the war was hundreds of miles and years away and we weren't in No Man's Land any more. We weren't just a swim away from Albion.

We were in paradise.

FIRE

Hours we swam for, or it felt it. Launching in off a rope swing, then further out off the boat. Until our fingers were shrivelled and our bellies growling for food.

'Doesn't Noah swim?' I asked as we waded towards the bank.

'Not here,' Poppy explained. 'Says it's for savages.'

And I should have been angry, but it made me proud somehow. 'Savages!' I shouted across the river, my hand cupped round my mouth, so all of Albion might hear.

Leon laughed, put both his hands up and hollered too, then started to dance, splashing in the shallows so it sent muddy sludge up his own legs and ours. I didn't mind. But Poppy did.

'All right,' she said. 'Not that savage.'

'Sorry,' I said, clutching my hands round myself. It was all right in the water, under the sun, but the trees made it feel like winter suddenly. I began to shiver.

'Fire?' said Poppy, pulling her hair back and wringing it like a wet rag.

Leon shook himself off like a dog then looked at her and nodded. 'Fire,' he agreed.

They built it weird – not like on the TV shows – but upside down. Big logs at the bottom, then smaller then twigs for kindling and a bit of paper from the sack.

'How will you start it?' I asked. 'Will you rub a stick on a stone?'

Poppy snorted, pulled something silver and glinting from her pocket, like a set of shapeless keys.

'What's that?'

'Flint,' she said, striking the keys against each other like she was sharpening them.

Whatever it was, it worked. Off flew a tiny spark into a shrivel of paper, and Leon – more careful than

I'd ever seen him – blew on that until it smoked before setting it in place. It took a second but then the kindling crackled and a thin flame licked into the twigs and before long we were warm and dry and stinking of wood smoke.

'Here,' said Poppy then, opening the sack and pulling out a bag.

'Marshmallows!' shouted Leon, as if he were no more than Sam's age, as if he hadn't just lit a fire seconds ago, like the man he really was.

Though I knew why he felt it. I'd not seen marshmallows – not seen any sweets – since I'd got here.

'Where'd you get them?' I asked. 'John?'

She nodded. 'Don't know where *he* got them from though, and I don't want to know either.'

Albion, I thought. *He got them in Albion.*

But who cared? I hadn't had a treat in weeks and here they were, toasting on sticks on a fire until the edges blackened and the insides pooled into sugary goop.

I ate ten.

Between us we finished the bag and sat staring into orange embers until Poppy said we'd better get the rest of the stuff back before Julia sent out a search party.

Leon stood quick at that, poured river water on the fire to dampen the ashes.

Then the three of us, sun-drunk and swum-out, made our slow and silent way back to the house. To Sam and Minnow. To Maggie and Mr Minton. To Julia and Noah.

And to someone else.

Leon saw him first, stopped dead in his tracks and mumbled something that sounded like the worst swear.

Poppy stopped and all. 'Oh,' she said. 'Oh.'

'What?' I asked. 'Who is it?'

'That,' she said, stilted and bristling, 'is my dad.'

MR GRAYSON

I don't know what I'd thought her and Noah's dad might look like. But whatever I could have come up with, it wouldn't be this.

He was tall, like them. But there was nothing of the country about him. Nothing free. Nothing tree-loving. He didn't even have Noah's stringy ease. He was smart and stiff and his face was grim, even when Noah flung himself at him in a hug.

'That's enough,' the man said, pushing Noah away. 'You're not a girl, for God's sake.'

Noah's face went strange then, and he mumbled a 'sorry' or something like it.

'Jesus,' said Julia. 'You're not the one who needs to apologise, Noah.' She turned to the man. 'I told you not to come.'

'And I told you it wasn't up to you. They're my children.'

Julia laughed, but not the happy kind.

Poppy said nothing. Did nothing.

The man put his hands on his hips, like he was waiting for something. And I saw it then, on the inside of his arm, same as Mr Metcalfe.

He was an Albioneer.

'Come along.' Maggie ushered us. 'Inside, now.'

It was me and Sam she was talking to. Minnow and Leon had already sloped off, to the rabbits most likely.

'But . . .' I began, looking at Poppy. What if she needed me? I swung my head. What if Noah needed me? 'It's—'

'No buts,' said Maggie. 'None of your business, that's what it is.'

That. Again. I was sick of it.

But inside we had to sit, while over the yard the

man – Mr Grayson, Maggie told us – hissed things and then shouted things and then slammed the door of his car and drove off up the lane.

When I looked out Poppy was still standing there, watching the dust of him. But Noah was gone, the door to the house slamming behind him, Julia following, trying to reason with him, though I couldn't tell why.

I stood to go but Maggie pulled me back again.

'Leave them,' she said. 'It's always like this. He'll calm down by the morning.'

'What about Poppy?'

'Poppy's not so bothered as her brother.'

I didn't understand. That didn't make sense. 'You mean she's not bothered her dad's an Albioneer?'

Maggie looked at me funny. 'No,' she said. 'Not so bothered he's gone.'

THE CONFESSION
(three days until D-Day)

I didn't see Noah the next day. Poppy told me not to even try looking for him, because he didn't want to be found and I wouldn't want to find him anyway because he'd be in such a bad mood.

'Why?' I asked. 'Is he angry at him? At your dad, I mean. For . . .' I didn't know to say it. 'For being, you know. One of them.'

Poppy looked at me. 'You don't know anything,' she said. And then she was gone as well, off with the women, I reckoned, two of them round Julia's, shut in the kitchen, whispering about stuff. Women's stuff.

They were there the next day as well, and I was tired of being by myself. Tired of milking in silence, tired of watching Sam and Minnow and Leon in their own weird world. Like a bunch of Marvel misfits, only without the special powers. Because that's what No Man's Land was. No superheroes. No chosen ones. Just a bunch of women up to something and us lot with no idea what.

That's why I had to see him. Noah, I mean. Because he was a boy. Because he knew what it meant to be left behind. Because he knew what it meant to be without your dad. Even if his was an Albioneer.

***

He was in the folly, like I knew he would be. Hiding out with his knife and his wood and a bag of peanuts.

'You all right?' I asked.

He looked up. 'Oh, you,' he said. Like I was the worst disappointment.

But I wasn't giving in. So I sat down opposite him and watched as he whittled.

He didn't say anything, didn't even look at me. But after a while he nudged the bag over with his foot.

I took one, cracked open the papery shell and let

the two red nuts roll into my hand and then into my mouth.

'Did your dad bring you these?' I said.

I thought I was being clever. Saying it casually. But Noah just stared at me like I was stupid.

'He's got better things to do.'

Then I remembered – the sack, John's contraband. I *was* stupid.

'My dad's miles away, too,' I tried.

'What do you know about it?' he said. 'What do you know about anything?'

'I—'

'You don't even know war's coming, do you? In ten days. Ninth of August.'

My insides jinked. 'They didn't make an agreement?'

'With Europe? Europe won't agree to anything.'

'Did your dad tell you that?'

He nodded. 'He's signed up. Being packed off somewhere exciting. And we're stuck here.'

'I thought this was supposed to be safe?' Isn't that why Dad had sent us?

'Safe?' He snorted. 'How's it safe?'

'I don't . . . I don't know.'

'No army. No nothing,' he carried on. 'What are we supposed to do? I want to *do* something. I want to fight! Not sit around listening to women say it would all be better if they ran the world. It wouldn't anyway. They hate us. They'll make us their slaves. If they don't throw us out first.'

'What?' I didn't get it. 'They wouldn't do that.'

'Oh, wake up,' he spat. 'They don't even want John, do they? It'll be me next.'

'But Mr Minton—'

'He'll be dead soon. And Leon's not all there.' He tapped his head then; code for 'stupid'. 'So he doesn't count either. And you want to watch yourself and all.'

Leon wasn't stupid, not one bit, and I got that buzz in me, a sicky sort of fizz. But I knew it was pointless saying anything, so I swallowed it down. 'I'm going home,' I said, steady as I could.

'In your dreams. You're one of us now. Doing nothing. Like me.'

I thought of that afternoon, before his dad showed up, thought of me and Poppy and Leon swimming in the river – wild boys and girls, free as the fish. 'There *are* things,' I said. 'To do, I mean. Swim, for instance, and . . . and—'

'Swim?' He snorted. 'I don't want to bloody swim, like a nobody. I want to be *some*body. I want to be a hero. But how can I? Don't even know where to go to do it. Haven't got a phone. Haven't got a computer. And my knife's only good for wood and rabbits.' He flung it to the floor then, kicked it for good measure.

And the thing is, I knew how he felt, I really did. Swimming was one thing, but I didn't want to be nobody. I didn't want to be one of Dad's 'ordinary people'. I wanted to be a hero too. Not for Albion, but for The Rest of the World or the Resistance, whoever they were, or just for Someone. And I could feel it then – my secret. Gleaming inside me like a jewel, primed like a weapon. Because it *was* one, wasn't it?

It was a gun.

And I wanted to give it to him, like a present.

But then I thought of Maggie, arms crossed, staring at me. Could feel her in the air around me making it tight and tense – even more than it was with Noah.

And I couldn't do it. Couldn't hand it to him after all. Because it wasn't mine to give.

But I could do this: 'I understand,' I said. 'I miss the old world too.'

And not a word of that was a lie.

Noah picked a peanut, cracked it open and checked the nuts into his mouth. 'Thanks,' he said.

Then he snatched up his knife from the dirt, dusted it off, and went back to his whittling.

***

'Can I have the phone?' I begged Maggie soon as I got back.

'Keep your hair on,' she said. 'All in good time.'

'No, now!' I snapped. And guilt was a wash of cold but it didn't stop me. 'Please!'

Maggie stared at me. But she got it, while Mr Minton muttered on about manners and modern

ways and how the world might as well end. Idiot.
It *was* ending.

And that's why I needed Dad more than ever.
Needed him to come. To fix things just by being
there, like dads are meant to.

I texted him. Punched it in quick. **DPNF OPX**
And waited.

And waited.

And waited.

But the phone sat in Maggie's hand sullen and
silent and black. Right through tea, right through
the game of snap she made me and Sam have, even
though I didn't want to and Sam cheated anyway,
and right through to bed.

'Will you wake me?' I said as she pulled the duvet
up over me. 'If he texts.'

'If he texts,' she said. 'I'll wake you.'

SILENCE
(two days until D-Day)

But she didn't wake me. Because he didn't text.

I got up at six, with the clatter of chickens and the sunlight seeping through the thread of the drapes and the phone stubborn as Shirley in one of her moods. Refusing to move. Refusing to do anything.

'You're sure you haven't deleted it by mistake?' I asked.

'Surprised you think I know how,' Maggie replied. 'But no.'

He's just busy, I told myself. Because of the war coming. Because of cracking all the codes.

But as soon as I'd said that, even silently, I felt sick again.

'Go on out,' said Maggie. 'You'll feel better then.'

So I did go out.

But I didn't feel better. I was jittery, ill even. My stomach too tight to eat anything, my legs twitching with need.

Not even Poppy could cheer me up.

'Remember I said we could have a party?' She nudged me. 'For your birthday, I mean.'

'Party,' repeated Leon, who was sitting with us on the wall, legs dangling, his eyes on Sam and Minnow playing with Dave in the dirt of the yard.

'I don't want a party,' I snapped back. 'I just want my dad.'

'He's probably busy,' said Poppy. 'John's busy, isn't he, Leon?'

Leon nodded, let his dangling legs bash against the wall. 'Busy,' he repeated, his feet sounding the rhythm into the brick. 'Bu-sy, bu-sy, bu-sy.'

Busy. Same as I'd told myself. But look where that had got me. *Nowheresville*, Ahmed would say.

Ahmed. Where was he now? Was he even still in Brigstowe?

But I couldn't think of him or Dad so I changed

the subject. 'Why're all the women here again?'

They were in Julia's kitchen, door shut, Maggie in with them and all. Their voices soaring then sinking, swears like commas, hoots of laughter like full stops.

She shrugged. 'Meetings,' she said. Like that meant anything.

'They're not talking normally,' I pointed out. 'It's not English. 'Cept the swearing.'

'It's Kernewek,' said Poppy.

'Is that even a language?'

'No, I just made it up.' Poppy rolled her eyes. ''Course it is.'

I pulled a face back. 'But why?'

'So you can't understand,' said Noah, who'd loped into the yard to fetch a bucket and some straw before loping off again, keeping himself to himself more than ever.

'Ignore him,' said Poppy. 'I do.'

But I couldn't ignore him, could I? Not totally. Any more than I could ignore the fact that Dad hadn't got back to me.

***

Maggie handed me the phone after dinner, before I'd even asked.

'Can't I just ring him?' I said.

She shook her head. 'You know you can't.'

''Cause of the ears in the walls!' said Sam.

'Shut up,' I said.

'Hey!' snapped Maggie. 'No need for that.'

What did she care? She didn't even like boys. And it didn't matter all the farting stuff, she still wished we were girls, I knew it.

And I could just do it anyway. Could just call him and beg him to fetch us right now. But something stopped me.

Sense, Dad would have said.

Or fear, more likely. Of him answering and then getting caught and taken away.

Or him not answering at all.

So I just texted the same again:

DPNF OPX

And I texted the same again two hours later.

And two hours after that.

And the next morning.

And each time came the same reply:
A big fat nothing.

RESISTANCE
(one day until D-Day)

August 2nd and August 9th.

My birthday and war.

Those two dates sat on the calendar ringed in red, like they were fire-hot and dangerous, one sizzling above the other.

And to think when I marked my date, that was all that mattered. That was the day everything would go back to normal. But I wasn't even sure my dad was coming and even if he did, the second red circle would just get fatter and more menacing until it swallowed the first one and any good would disappear in one massive snap.

Or a bomb.

And all the time we just sat around whittling

things, and milking goats, and feeding rabbits like nothing was happening. Like it was just another ordinary day in an ordinary world. And we were ordinary people.

And I hated it. I hated being one of them.

And the more I thought about it, the more I understood Noah and his own sizzling anger at this place. He wanted to *do* something.

And I realised it more than ever: so did I.

I wanted to be a hero. Not Superman or Iron Man or any Man in a cape or tights or a fancy suit. But someone real. Someone who made a difference to ordinary lives.

And then it came to me, big and gleaming. Someone like the Resistance!

Only, who *were* the Resistance?

No one seemed to know anything. Least of all Maggie.

Sam had asked her, see.

'Do they look like normal people?' he asked at tea. 'With noses and stuff.'

Maggie rolled her eyes and tore a piece of bread

before poking it in her mouth. 'I suppose so,' she said, chewing at the same time so I could see it all churning like a cement mixer.

'But with X-ray brains?' Sam went on.

'I doubt it.'

'What about lasers?' he tried. 'In their fingers.'

'No.'

'Or exploding eyeballs?'

Mr Minton snorted.

Maggie sighed. 'They're just . . . normal.' She shrugged. 'Like you and me.'

I seized on it then, had the gun in my head, shining like bright evidence. 'Like you?' I said. 'Are you Resistance, then? Are you going to fight?'

Maggie snorted, and a glob of bread shot on to the table. She brushed it off. 'That what you reckon?' she said. 'That I've got some kind of underground racket going on?' Her laugh was knife-sharp and just as painful.

'In what?' I snapped. 'Doing nothing?'

Maggie stared then, as if I were thick as Jayden Nesbitt, and that was almost as bad as the slicing laugh. But then something in her softened. 'We're not doing nothing. This' – she flung her hands in the air as if she was taking in the whole of not just Tamar but No Man's Land – 'isn't nothing.'

But I wasn't having it. 'But what does it do?'

'Do?'

'What's it for? What's the point of being . . . nothing? Being in the middle.'

She paused for a moment. 'Being neutral means we're somewhere safe.'

'But for who? Who does it save?'

'So far? Maybe not many. Me. And Leon. And Mr Minton, maybe.'

He made a noise then, as if to say yes.

And that wasn't nothing. But I thought about Alan Turing stopping the war and saving millions of lives. 'That's not enough,' I said.

'Is that so?'

And I knew she was testing me. But if I was going to be any kind of hero, I couldn't break now, not after only a minute or so.

'It is so,' I said. 'It definitely is.'

And for a minute I shimmered, and Dad and my birthday were shrunk into nothing, and I felt what I reckoned all heroes before me had felt: that they were part of something bigger than them, more important than them.

But then Sam spilt his milk and it spread across the table and dripped down on to my trousers.

'Alan weed himself!' he yelped triumphantly.

'Oh, shut up,' I snapped as I stood up, my chair clattering to the floor behind me. 'Shut up, all of you.'

And I stamped up the stairs and slammed my door and threw myself on the bed that smelt of here, and I didn't even bother to text Dad again because what was the point?

What was the point in anything any more?

D-DAY

'Happy birthday, Alan,' Maggie said at breakfast.

'It's not,' I said.

'Not your birthday?' said Sam.

'Not happy,' I said, and slumped down in my chair.

Maggie raised her eyebrows but she didn't tell me off. Because she knew I was right.

'Wait until tonight,' she said. 'Big party.'

'With cake?' asked Sam. 'And presents?'

'With cake,' said Maggie.

Mr Minton muttered.

I shrugged. What did I care about a party? Or presents?

The only thing I wanted was my dad. And there was no sign of him showing up. Not a word.

'Maybe it's a surprise,' said Poppy when we were milking. 'Maybe he'll just come.'

'Has he rung your mum, then?' I asked, yanking on Shirley's teat.

'No, but—'

'So how would he even get here with no boat? That's just— Ow!'

Shirley had kicked me and knocked the bucket with it, milk pooling thin and pale on the floor.

'Sorry,' I said.

'Doesn't matter,' said Poppy.

But I knew she was lying. Everything mattered. Every little scrap mattered. Leftovers were made into meals the next day or, at worst, fed to the animals. Nothing was wasted.

Waste not, want not.

And the thought of Mum then was needle-sharp and pricking. The thought of Dad as bad.

'Here,' said Poppy then, holding out her hand as I tried to mop up my mess.

'What's that?'

'Take it.'

I propped the mop against the wall, took the packet wrapped in brown paper and tied with nettle thread. I opened it in one pull, and there, nestled, was a bead. On it, in looping black ink, the letter A. For Alan.

'You tie it on with the thread,' said Poppy. 'Here.'

And she poked one end through the wooden bead and then hung it around my neck.

I didn't know what to say. I'd never had a necklace before. Least not since the pasta ones Sam came home from nursery with and made me wear. But I'd seen Poppy and Minnow with them. P and M round their necks. Even Leon. Even Noah, when I'd first got here anyway. He'd stopped wearing it in the last few days.

'Where'd you get it?' I asked.

'I made it,' she said. 'From elder.'

I nodded, fingering the wooden bead, rolling it round and round. 'Thanks,' I said.

'You're one of us now,' she said.

And I should have been happy at that. Should

have smiled to be included, because that's what Mrs King always wanted from us – to include everyone in our groups. To stop singling each other out like Jayden Nesbitt had done, for being too tall or too short or too anything. Because being included felt like a hug. Felt like being one big family. Least that's what she said.

But this didn't feel like a hug. It didn't feel like I was part of one big family.

It felt like I was losing my old one.

**

I got other things too. I didn't expect anything from Maggie. But I got pictures from Sam and Minnow and Leon. 'Rabbits,' said Sam. As if I couldn't see. 'Harry Potter and Hermione and Dave.'

I got my own flint from Julia. 'So you'll always be warm and always be fed,' she said.

And I got a bag of marshmallows from John.

'Thanks,' I said. 'But I'm not really hungry.'

'That's OK,' said John. 'You can toast them at the party later.'

But I didn't feel hungry then either.

So I watched as Leon and Minnow and Sam packed them in their mouths playing some game called 'chubby bunnies'.

Watched John play guitar while Poppy and Julia whirled in circles, mirrors in their skirts like tiny flickers of fire.

Watched Maggie and Mr Minton drink cloudy beer and clink bottles with no labels.

Past bedtime.

Past seven, past eight, past nine, past ten.

Until Julia said we'd had enough and there was work to do in the morning and time and tide waited for no man, which was code for having to get on with stuff.

I picked up my flint and my pictures when I felt a hand on my shoulder. For a second I brimmed with hope. But then I saw the fingers were too skinny and there was no hair on them, no silver ring.

'Noah,' I said.

He'd been skulking at the party, not joining in with anything. Just sitting on the wall flicking bits of moss off with his knife. Poppy had told me to ignore him. So I had. But I couldn't now, not with his fingers gripping me.

'Tomorrow at the folly,' he said.

'What?'

'You heard. Come to the folly at four. I've got something for you.'

'A present?' I said.

He stared at me, his eyes orange in the firelight. 'Something like that.'

I nodded. 'All right,' I said. 'Four.'

When I went in, Maggie was at the sink, her hands deep in the water, swilling off the plates from dinner. More food that I'd not eaten.

She looked up. 'I'm sorry,' she said.

'For what?'

She took her hands out of the water, wiped them on a tea towel.

'Your dad,' she said.

I nodded.

And then she opened her arms. And I didn't know what she was doing at first. She just stood there, like some sort of scarecrow. Then I got it.

She was offering me a hug. An actual one.

And for a second I teetered, my feet twitching, like I was on a rollercoaster on the top of the track and might plunge down any second, barrel right into her.

But then I snapped to. Remembered myself. Remembered the walls had ears – and eyes and all, probably. Remembered that villains didn't come in cackling madly and flashing their tattoos. They came in pretending to be your friend. And even if she wasn't a villain, what was she actually doing to help? What kind of hero did she think she was?

'Night,' I said. And trudged up to bed.

THE TATTOO
(one day after D-Day, six days before war)

When I got to the folly and pushed open the wooden door, I saw Noah had already prepared: a cloth on the floor, the knife and a bottle of black ink laid out on it.

I knew what was going on, what he meant to do. Didn't need to ask.

'I don't think I want one after all,' I said, trying to sound as if it was a casual decision.

He swore then. A bad one. Then added, 'Why not?'

'Just' – I snatched at something Mum had said, when Dad wanted a duck inked on his arm – 'it's supposed to mean something. And a sword doesn't mean anything to me.'

'I thought we were the same, me and you.'

'We are,' I said, and it was only half a lie.

'Don't you want to stand out? Be someone?'

'I do,' I insisted, and that was all truth.

He stood then so I could see the height of him, feel it too, towering like he was Goliath and I was nothing.

'What?' I whispered.

Then he did something weird. He pulled down the side of his shorts. Not far, just an inch or so. But far enough so I could see.

I felt a gasp come out of me before I could stop it. Because there it was in thick black ink. Same as Mr Metcalfe. Same as his dad.

'Why?' I managed.

He pulled up his shorts. 'Who do you think's going to protect you from Europe when the war comes? Your dad?'

'I . . .'

'Why do you s'pose he's not come for you? What do you think he's up to?'

A bucket of cold water sloshed through my insides. 'I . . . I don't know,' I admitted. Then mimicked Poppy, Leon: 'Busy, I think.'

'Signed up, more likely. Or conscripted.'

I felt weaker than ever. Weak as Jayden Nesbitt said I was. 'What's conscripted?' I managed.

'Made to join up, even if you don't want to. Even if you're a chicken.'

'My dad's not a chicken!'

'No? What is he then? A Traitor?' He snapped the word out like a bullet, hard, so it hurt when it hit.

'No!' I yelped. 'He works in code. He cracks codes. It's . . . it's important.'

Noah shook his head. 'So he's a spy then. Like Maggie.'

I didn't understand. 'Maggie's not a spy,' I said. 'She's nobody. She told me herself.'

'You don't know that. You don't know anything. How do you think she knew about the war, hey?'

I thought about it then – that red ring on the

calendar – she'd known before any of us about war coming. And I thought about her always being up to something after all. Always sneaking about. Snooping through my messages.

Then it hit me. She hadn't just snooped through them. She'd read them. Even though I'd used the Caesar shift.

She knew code.

My gut felt like it was being swept up my gullet. Had she lied about not being Resistance? And if she had, was that bad like Noah said, or good?

I swallowed hard.

'They're fooling you,' he said. 'They all are. Pretending to like you. Pretending to help you. But they're liars. All of them. All of them on the other side.'

'What side?' I said, desperate.

He looked at me, shook his head. 'The wrong one.'

I didn't say anything. Couldn't. Because I didn't know what was right or wrong or truth or lies any more. I thought they were just doing nothing, but maybe that was a lie as well.

'Anyway, I'm not waiting around to get caught out.'

'What do you mean?'

'I'm out of here. Soon as I can.'

My insides were alive then, as if electricity was fizzing through my veins instead of blood, as if a ball of it were stuck in my stomach.

'Where will you go?'

'After my dad if I can. If not, wherever'll have me.'

'What will you do?'

He laughed. 'Are you an idiot? I'll fight, won't I. I'll make a difference.'

And even though I knew he meant for Albion, I knew something else too: we were the same, me and him. We didn't want to just sit around. We wanted to make our mark.

And we wanted our dads and all.

'Take me with you,' I begged.

'What?' Noah pulled a face like I was mental. Perhaps I was. 'Why should I?'

'I can help. I can ... give you stuff?'

'Like what? Your penknife?' He laughed, short and hard.

'I know code,' I tried.

'What code? From the old wars? What good's that now? It's all computers.'

'I . . .' I snatched in the air for ideas as if they were flies. But they were too quick for me, too small. Not even worth chasing.

Except . . .

'There's a gun,' I blurted.

Noah met my eyes, stuck his knife, blade down, in the ground. 'What?'

'Maggie,' I said. 'She's got a gun. I've seen it.'

'Where? Where've you seen it?'

He was leaning in at me now, so close I could see the red rims of his eyes, the flare of his nose, the scar on his cheek.

'The pantry,' I said.

'Where in the pantry?' He'd got hold of me now, the collar of my T-shirt tight in his fist.

'Next to the washing machine. Please don't hurt me,' I begged.

He let go and I slumped into the mud.

'You better not be lying.'

'I'm not,' I said, brushing dust off me, my heart still fast as a rabbit's. 'I promise.'

Noah nodded.

'So you'll take me then?'

Noah said nothing.

'You can tattoo me.' I pulled up my sleeve and held out my bare arm. 'Whatever you like. I don't mind.'

But Noah pulled his knife out of the ground, flipped the blade back into the carved wooden sheath. 'Maybe tomorrow,' he said.

'Tomorrow,' I repeated, trying not to show my relief.

Tomorrow.

***

Poppy stopped me when I got back.

'Where've you been?' she asked. 'I was looking for you.'

'Nowhere,' I said, that sick feeling washing through me again. 'Just . . . with Noah.'

She frowned. 'You want to be careful,' she said. 'You're . . . different to him.'

'No, I'm not,' I said, my jaw hard and forward. 'Not so much as you think, anyway.'

Poppy frowned. 'I'm on your side,' she said then. 'You know that, don't you?' And she touched my cheek with her fingers, held them there like they were healing.

And for a second they were – hot like the spark from a flint, like the crackle of kindling, sending a rush of something through me.

But then I heard Noah. 'She *would* say that, *wouldn't* she.'

So how could I believe her? How could I believe anyone any more? Not even my dad had told the truth. Because he was there and I was here.

But maybe not for long.

I brushed her hand off. 'I've got to go,' I said.

'Go where?'

But I was in the house and up the stairs before I'd even tried to think of a lie.

THE BULLET
(three days after D-Day,
four days before war)

But tomorrow never came.

'Cause the day after, I stayed out of his way. And the day after that, he stayed out of everyone's.

For good.

***

'Where is it?'

I opened my eyes and there she was. Maggie. Her face in mine, her mouth open and her breath coffee-sour and hot.

'What?' I groaned – it felt early still, too early for milking.

'You know what,' she said.

And at once I pictured it. The gun. And I felt a bullet

through my body, springing me awake and sending my stomach spinning.

'I know you know about it.'

'I don't,' I lied.

'You do,' she said. 'Mr Minton said you'd been snooping about. It doesn't take much to put two and two together.'

I was upright by then, peering round her for Sam, checking he wasn't scared by the racket. But his bed was already empty, the covers yanked back – off with the rabbits probably. Or Leon at least.

'Tell me,' she said.

I knew what had happened. Knew he must've got it already, stashed it someplace for our escape. So snitching on him would mean snitching on me too. And ruining everything. 'I can't,' I said.

'Can't or won't?'

I knew she could see the lie inside me then. Lit up like it was written in neon. 'It wasn't me that took it,' I said.

'So who was it then? The Queen of Sheba?'

That was code. For nobody. For a lie.

But I wasn't lying, not this time. It's just that I couldn't tell the truth.

But I didn't have to. Because right then Sam screamed. A scream so loud it made Mr Minton shout from downstairs that the 'bloody kids were up to no bloody good again'. And I felt sick then, scared that Sam had got shot. And I ran after Maggie, still in my pyjamas, ramming my feet into my too-small boots before bursting out the door.

But Sam wasn't hurt; Leon and Minnow neither.

'What's going on?' said Julia, still in her nightie herself.

'Harry Potter's gone,' wailed Minnow, her hand wedged in Sam's.

Leon moaned, a low animal sound that made me shudder.

'He's probably just got loose,' said Julia. 'You probably forgot to lock the cage last night.'

Leon moaned again. Sam screamed.

'We didn't,' pleaded Minnow. 'We locked it proper.'

'Where's Noah?' said Poppy, all of a sudden.

Maggie and Julia looked at each other and

I knew then that it was their own silent grown-up code. And I knew in my fast heart and sickly stomach what had happened.

'Alan?' asked Maggie.

'I . . .'

I didn't want to tell. But Sam was crying now, fat tears making rivers through his dusty cheeks, and Leon was moaning, low and cow-like. And maybe . . . maybe we didn't need the gun anyway. We could say it was just for practise in the woods. For catching . . . pheasants or deer or whatever other weird meat Maggie ate. And—

'The folly,' I said. 'Try the folly.'

***

Julia made Minnow and Sam stay with Leon, but Poppy and Maggie and me all ran through the woods, stamping on scattered hazelnuts, tripping over roots of trees, bare and spreading like skeletons. It seemed further than before, taking for ever to get there. Me wishing I was faster, wishing I was quick as a fish. Or a superhero.

But when we got to the folly I wished I'd not

been able to shift at all. Because there, nailed to the gaping door, blood on its fur and its eyes glassy and black, was the rabbit.

Even though I'd not eaten, I could feel sick creeping up my gullet and I had to swallow hard.

Poppy grabbed at my hand and I didn't stop her, let her fingers twine around mine, even though this was my fault.

'He's gone, then,' said Maggie.

Julia'd had her hand over her mouth until then, holding something in. But then she dropped it, let the words burst out. 'He's got a gun, for God's sake, Maggie! A kid with a bloody gun.'

'Julia—' Maggie tried to hush her.

But Julia wouldn't be hushed. 'I knew it was a mistake. You keeping it in the first place. Keeping it in the open. Why wasn't it locked like everything else?'

Poppy dropped my hand, went to her mum, threaded her arms around her. Though Julia's arms stayed hanging by her side, useless, as if they were broken.

Even so, at least Poppy had someone. And I wanted my dad then, so badly. Wanted him to fix everything.

Why hadn't Noah waited so he could take me to him?

And why'd he done this?

And I could feel my own tears come, and snot and all, had to wipe them away. 'Where is he?' I asked. 'Where'd he go?'

'Huh?' Maggie turned to me.

'Noah,' I snapped. 'Where's he gone?'

But I knew the answer before Maggie said it. 'After his dad, I expect.'

I looked at Julia, thin and pale and ghost-like in her white nightie. And I wanted to say I was sorry, I did.

But I was mostly sorry for me and that stoppered up the words like they were stones in my throat.

Because he'd lied. He'd taken my one prize and left me here to do nothing with the women while over the border, war was starting and my dad was doing who knew what.

'We could go after him,' I said, desperate. 'We could follow him and . . . and trap him and . . . and bring him back.' *And I could just stay there and find my own dad*, I didn't add.

Julia shook her head, opened her mouth to let quiet words out. Kind, in spite of it. 'He's sixteen in a week. He can do as he likes.'

'You can't tell him anything, anyway,' added Maggie. 'Never could.'

Poppy made a noise that I knew meant she agreed.

'So that's it?' I said.

'For now,' said Maggie.

And even though she said it like it was nothing, I could see even her eyes were wet and red round the edges and I knew she was keeping in tears, saving them for later when Julia was gone, perhaps.

'I'm sorry,' I said.

'It's not your fault,' said Julia.

It was though. I knew it. In every cell of me.

And so did they, I reckoned.

'Right,' Maggie said then, nodding at Julia.

'Work to be done.'

Julia took a breath. Wiped her face. Then peeled Poppy from round her. 'Work,' she said.

But my feet wouldn't move, so I was stuck there, heard it all. Heard the terrible wrenching sound and looked round to see Maggie yanking the rabbit off the nail. My stomach churned as a bit of bloody fur got stuck, as Harry Potter hung limp in her hand.

'What are you doing?' I asked quietly.

'It's only an hour or so dead,' she said. 'Waste not, want not.'

And before I could breathe deep, I threw up – a hot arc of sick spattering on the red of my boots.

If this was normal, I didn't want any of it.

BELLY

It was Julia who cleaned me up when we got back. Wiped my face clean, changed my clothes for me, gave me a top of Noah's 'cause 'the rest of mine were looking a bit grim', she said.

'Dad didn't have time to wash them,' I said. 'He's been busy. With . . . important stuff.' With what? With something, anyway.

'I know,' she said as she looked me up and down like she was sizing me up.

'It doesn't fit,' I said, pushing the sleeves up my arms. Then, softer. '*I* don't fit.'

She stared at me, then frowned. 'Oh, love.'

'I'm not supposed to be here. I—'

'You are,' she interrupted. 'You are.' And she was certain, as sure of it as if it was the sun coming up in the morning or the earth turning.

'But—'

'You know we've met before?' she said then.

I peered at her, at the glints of pink in her burgundy hair. The slivers of silver in her skirt – tiny mirrors that caught the sun.

'At the funeral,' she prompted.

I shook my head. 'I . . . I don't remember,' I said.

'Don't suppose you remember a lot from back then,' she said.

I shrugged. Fourteen things. Fifteen now. But what did that matter?

'You know she came here?'

I shook my head. I didn't know that. Dad had never said. Dad never said anything much though.

'You too.'

'What?' I didn't understand.

'In her belly, mind. But you were here, all the same.'

Something flipped in me. Like a piece of a puzzle trying to slip into place. But no – I stopped it dead – even if she'd been here, even if *I'd* been here, didn't mean I was supposed to be here now. Didn't mean this was right, any of it.

'I should go,' I said then. 'Work, you know?'

She stared at me a second longer then nodded. 'Go on,' she said.

I took a breath. 'I'm sorry about Noah,' I added. 'He'll come back.'

She smiled, but the weak kind that's mainly sad. 'Maybe,' she said. 'Maybe not.'

And I knew I should hug her, knew that there were tears just inside her eyes again, waiting to flood out.

But something in me was cold and hard and cross and so instead I just turned and walked out the door dressed in her runaway son's too-big T-shirt.

And I wondered where he was. How far into Albion now.

And despite everything he'd done, I wished I wished I wished I was with him.

THE PLAN

After that everything went back to normal. Or normal for here. As if nothing had happened. Goats had to be milked. Rabbits – the ones left – had to be cleaned. Wood had to be chopped and now it was Poppy's job to fetch it, to stack it, even to use the axe. And the day still tick-tocked round like it did before, everyone doing their bit, until dinner time.

I didn't go down to eat. Even though Julia had made me and Sam sandwiches so we didn't have to have Harry Potter stew. I could smell it from my bedroom though, meaty and savoury and dead. And my head filled thick with thoughts then. Of Noah. Of his dad. Of Albion.

Of *my* dad.

And it hit me then. Dad wasn't a hero. He wasn't

coming to rescue me. He was too busy, like Maggie said. Being a nobody. Or a chicken, like Noah claimed. But even if he was a chicken, that didn't mean *I* had to stay, did it? That didn't mean I had to do nothing. Be a nobody. So I wasn't Noah; I didn't have a gun. But I had guts, I reckoned. And perhaps that was enough.

And that thought glimmered in the dimness, diamond-bright and precise. Because I could go home. I could take Sam and I could go home. Get there before war started. Before Dad got consigned or whatever it was. Then Albion'd have to change their minds because he'd have a responsibility, wouldn't he? They'd have to spare him. Or if not, well, *we* could be the Resistance. Me and Sam. We could fight, somehow. I knew code and Sam was clever enough, for a five year old.

We could leave easy as anything. I even knew the route – straight down the river to Plym Mouth then on to the train. We had papers as well; no one could stop us.

Could they?

But I squished the seed of doubt down as if it was no more than a dropped conker.

No, they couldn't stop us. All I needed now was for Maggie to go to bed and start her snoring. Then, like superheroes, like the Invisible Kid and Martian Manhunter, Sam and I would disappear – poof! Just like Noah.

And never come back.

PART 3: HOME

LEAVING NO MAN'S LAND

(three days after D-Day, four days before war)

I packed everything we needed. Not into the suitcases – we'd have to abandon them, along with most of our clothes – but into rucksacks from the pegs in the hallway, a big one for me and a smaller one for Sam: clean pants and socks for both of us, the penknife, the credit card Dad had given me for emergencies. Even my flint, not that I'd need that back in Albion. We had radiators there. Modern things. Proper things. I packed water as well, in two steel bottles – better for the environment, not that Albion cared about that now – and the sandwich I'd not eaten before, in case we couldn't find anything on the way.

Last of all, into my pocket I slipped the List.

Fifteen things on it now, more if I waited maybe, talked to Julia again. But no amount of waiting would bring my mum back, would it. And at least this way I might get to keep my dad.

I could barely breathe as I imagined knocking on our door on Bentley Street. Imagined hanging round Ahmed's, casual as anything, thrashing him at *Dino Crisis*. Imagined sticking a finger up at Paris to prove something. I wasn't sure what, but something. Thoughts of war, well, I pushed those out of my head. We still had three days left and anything might happen before then.

I was done but for one thing. The phone. I had to get it – in case Dad rang while we were on the way, and so I could let him know what we were doing. But the office was locked. So I waited until I could hear her – Maggie – the hee-haw of her snoring from the room at the end of the landing. And the rattle and clack of Mr Minton mithering in his sleep. Then I crept, soft and stealthy, down the stairs, along the corridor and to the study.

I'd not been in there before – the door was kept

shut in the day when Maggie was out, locked up with a key that she kept with a bunch of others in her pocket. But when she was in she stuck them in a drawer in the kitchen. I knew 'cause Leon sometimes got them out to mess with them. He liked the clanking of them in his hands. And Maggie would have to take them off him, swap them for a biscuit.

She should have locked them up and all. Like the gun. But perhaps she'd trusted us. Or just thought we were stupid. Whatever, I had them now, cold and tight in my fingers so they wouldn't make a sound.

It took me three goes to find the right one. Each time, my heart hammering so loud I thought she'd hear that if not the door. But then – click! – and I was in.

I didn't know why I'd not thought to try before, because here was all sorts of things: maps, plans, a globe of the world that spun on a stand. And something else and all: a strange machine, like a kind of a typewriter, only with wheels at the top and plugs at the bottom and wires criss-crossing between them.

I let out a breath of amazement. Because I knew

what it was – I'd seen one in a museum. Dad had explained it: it was from an old war, a machine to send code between the Nazis. The villains. The one that Alan Turing cracked.

It was an Enigma machine.

And I knew then that Noah was right. That Maggie might not be an Albioneer, but she was some kind of enemy. And I knew I was doing the right thing.

I hurried after that: slid open drawers and searched under papers, all the while careful not to rustle or knock or bang anything that might wake her. But still I couldn't see it, not even with my pocket torch on. *Maybe I'll have to abandon it*, I thought, take the risk anyway. But then I spied something – a shelf running round the panelling, crammed with ornaments: china dogs, old postcards, a photograph of Maggie, younger than now, her arm round another woman. *Laura*, I thought, remembering. Then more postcards, a pair of binoculars, a small tin jug.

And a black brick of a thing. Just sitting there for anyone to see.

A heave of relief went through me. I had

everything I needed now, and I reached out and grabbed it: my phone! My prize!

But before I could pocket it, I heard something – feet thudding on mud – and, my stomach fluttering, I swung my torch up to the window to see limbs skinny as twigs, hair pale as the moon, and the door of Julia's house slamming shut behind her.

Poppy.

Had she seen me? I couldn't be sure, but I couldn't be sure not, either. I just knew we had to go, and fast. Before she woke her mum or called the authorities – if they had them in Kernow – and they sent men after us. Or women, more likely. Because Noah – he was old enough to go. But me and Sam? We were kids. Eleven and five. And even though right then I felt big enough, felt clever and brave – a hero, even, despite what Dad said – I knew the women wouldn't agree.

So I steadied my legs, clicked off the torch, put the phone in my pocket.

And went to fetch Sam.

THE FLIGHT

'No,' moaned Sam, still thick with sleep.

'Please,' I begged. 'Please, just get up. We have to leave.'

'But why?'

'Because,' – I wracked my brains – 'because it's part of the Game.'

'Oh.' Sam sat up. 'OK.'

I couldn't believe he was so easily duped. Stupid, really – any villain could have persuaded him. But I didn't have time to tell him he needed to toughen up. I just needed him to get dressed.

It took longer than I'd planned, mainly because of the rabbits.

'Can I bring them?' he whispered.

We were hunched by the wall where we ate lunch.

'Don't be silly,' I whispered back. 'You can't take a bunch of rabbits on a train.'

He made a sad face, his bottom lip pushed out.

I groaned, but softly. 'You can say goodbye,' I said. 'If you're quick and quiet. I'll be lookout.'

Sam grinned at that. Because he knew the best games always have lookouts.

I kept my eyes on Maggie's house while Sam saw to the rabbits. I heard him click open the cage, mumble something, then click it shut again before hauling his rucksack on to his back. It was too big really, and I should have carried it all, but the water was heavy and I couldn't do everything. Besides, it was more authentic this way. The Game, I mean.

'Where now?' he said when he got back to the lookout.

'The river,' I said. 'Let's go.'

***

The woods were wild at night – all skittering insects and scampering animals and the flap of bats, quick and invisible. But on we marched, brave as anything, along the path where we skirted nettles and jumped skeleton roots, past the folly where I kept my eyes down so I couldn't see the nub of bloody fur, and on to the strip of beach where just days ago, I'd whooped and hollered and swum.

Sam stared at the boat like I was asking him to board a rocket.

'We're going in that?'

I nodded.

'You don't even know how to row,' he complained.

'I do too.'

'No, you don't,' said a voice that wasn't Sam's.

I gasped and looked up and there, on the edge of the trees, was Poppy.

Sickness swirled in my stomach. She *had* seen. I knew it.

'It's not what you think,' I blurted.

'It's the Game,' said Sam.

Poppy nodded. 'I know,' she said. 'And I want to play.'

I felt a shimmer in me. 'What?'

'I want to play,' she repeated. 'I mean, I want to come too.'

'But why?'

'Why do you think?' she said, as if it was obvious. 'To fetch Noah back.'

I frowned. 'Do you even know where he is?'

She shrugged. 'With my dad.'

'But—'

'And anyway,' she interrupted. 'How do you think you'll get to Plym Mouth without me?'

I squared up. 'Straight down the river,' I said. 'I'm not stupid.'

'Shows how much you know,' she said. 'What did you think? That you'd just moor up in the docks and they'd let you in?'

'I . . .'

'Kalstok,' she said. 'Then we walk the line.'

'The line?'

She nodded. 'The line.'

I thought for a moment. 'What makes you think they'd let *you* in, anyway?'

Poppy glared at me. 'What do you mean?'

'Well, you're a girl.'

'And?'

'Have you got papers?'

'No.'

'So if they stop you, which they will, looking like that' – I pointed at her hair – 'you're for it.'

'You could cut it,' said Sam. 'Cut it all off.'

'Don't be stupid,' I said.

'Don't call me stupid.'

I looked at him, fidgeting, on the brink of something. I couldn't risk it. 'Sorry,' I said quick. 'But she can't get a haircut here, can she.'

'Why not?' said Poppy suddenly. 'You've got scissors, haven't you?'

'What?'

'You said. On your penknife.'

'I . . .' But I did. I couldn't deny it. 'Yes,' I said.

'Then you'll have to do it for me.'

THE PENKNIFE
(four days after D-Day, three days before war)

I felt sick as I did it, my fingers shaking so much
I thought I'd snip an ear or my own skin.

'Just do it,' urged Poppy. 'Come on.'

'I'll try,' said Sam.

'No,' I said quick. I didn't want him injured.
I was to look after him – Dad had said. So I grabbed
a handful of hair – long it was, glinting and silvery
and so pretty I felt sick at what I was going to do.
But I was going to do it, I had to. And slowly, close
to the scalp, I snapped the scissors shut.

They didn't slice it straight and neat like
when the Turkish barbers did mine and Sam's
and Dad's on a Saturday before they got shut

down and we had to go Alf's in town. It was ragged and the ends were tufted up like feathers. But it was short and that was what mattered, wasn't it? I snipped another handful, and another, until it was gone.

'How do I look?' she asked.

I stared at her, all tufty, the skin underneath it glistening. 'Like Noah,' I said.

It was true, she did look like Noah. Only pretty.

Sam was mad with laughing.

Poppy pulled a face and I thought she was going to shout at me or cry even, because all her hair was gone and she looked like a chicken or a boy. But she just sighed. 'Well, that's good, isn't it? If I look like him?'

'I—'

'Because who'd stop me now?'

I shrugged. She was right. She could pass as a boy in her T-shirt and combat trousers. She didn't have big boobs or anything, like Maggie – not that I could tell anyway – so no one would wonder about those. And three of us was better than two, wasn't it? Three heroes. Doing something brave while everyone else just sat.

'You ready then?' she said, taking the boat's rope from the mooring hook.

I nodded. 'Ready.'

'Ready,' said Sam, though he was still fidgeting with his bag.

'Then let's go.'

***

The river was sleepy and still, only the shuffle of bulrushes and the splosh of oars in the water. On one side, Kalstok was a shut eye, no lights on, no hum of something – anything. On the other sat Albion, black and angry but silent. It was hard to believe war was close, then. But somewhere, miles up the train tracks, Londinium rumbled with it.

And time was running out.

We tied the boat up where we had before, so anyone would think we'd just gone to John's. But then, instead of turning right along the river, we took a left and walked up the hill.

At the top sat the railway station, the ticket office

boarded up, the platform cracked, tracks nettled and dead.

'We can't just jump down,' I said, toes on the faded yellow line, peering over the edge.

'We're going to have to.'

'But . . .'

I thought about the warnings at school. After Jayden Nesbitt's brother's mate got electrocuted larking about in Bedmelis. 'Stay off the lines,' Mrs Pritchard had said. 'They're live.'

But, 'Watch,' said Poppy. And she dropped down then, before I could stop her, stood on the metal of the rail.

I had to clamp a hand over my mouth to stop the yelp coming out. But then she turned and curtsied and alive as anything said, 'Come on.'

So we did.

I dropped to the floor first though, put my ear to the track to hear, like they did in films.

'There's nothing coming,' Poppy said. 'Hasn't been in years. And they shut off the electricity anyway.'

I listened harder. But she was right, there was nothing but the twisting of Sam's plimsolls as he tried to tightrope along it.

'How long?' I asked, standing up.

'By train? Ten minutes. On foot?' She shrugged. 'A few hours. We'll be there before dawn at least.'

In the ink of it, dawn felt days away. But I knew soon it'd spread its fingers across the hills to the east, and then eyes would open, the world would wake up.

'Come on then,' I said, hitching my rucksack up. 'Let's go.'

And left, right, left, right, we began to march into Albion.

ACROSS THE BORDER

We stopped for a moment, on top of the viaduct, one foot in No Man's Land, one in Albion. None of us told each other to, we just did it without thinking. All of us staring ahead, fizzing with it, like we were about to enter an enchanted forest or a dragon's lair.

Then, one by one – me in front, then Poppy, then Sam at the back – we crossed the border.

No thunder struck, no lightning cracked, no villains flew down from the sky.

It was no different, just gravel and tracks and trees a few metres into a place someone else had claimed. But even so we knew it wasn't the same. Nothing was the same now.

We passed through two more stations – both

of them boasting on posters about day trips to the sunshine coast, to a fancy mansion. Both of them derelict though. No day trippers for a decade; no trains to take them even if they did come.

'How do we know where to go?' asked Sam at one point.

'The track tells us,' replied Poppy. 'We just have to stick to it.'

'All the way?' I checked.

'Nearly,' she said. 'We'll duck off before we get to Plym Mouth though. Take the road then.'

'Oh,' said Sam, sounding disappointed, like he'd wanted to strike into the station like he was King of the Rails. Like he wouldn't be arrested straight away. Then, 'Wait.' And he hurried a few steps to catch up, like he had done for ages now.

I grabbed his hand to help him. 'How far?' I asked.

'Not far,' said Poppy.

'How will we know when we're nearly there?'

'Oh, you'll know,' she said. 'You'll know all right.'

***

It was the air more than anything. Not fresh any

more, not green-smelling, but gritty and grim and so thick you could slice it like cheese. City air, same as we had at home. So how had we not noticed it before? And the river was different here. Not a living thing, flanked by trees, but a wet wide murk, banks scattered with cranes and car parks, all lined up like Matchbox toys.

The houses looked different too – grey and terraced and clinging to hills as if they were bitter about it. Some of them granite, some of them pebble-dashed, a sick of stones stuck to their surface making them uglier still. Thin strings of yesterday's washing slung between them, life going on regardless.

One or two were painted – glimmers of blue and pink sticking out like sapphires and rubies, like they were defiant, like they were making a statement. And there was still some green – buddleia, Poppy told us, with the fat flowers dangling over the track like foxtails. Blackberries oozing their juice. No one bothering to pick them here. *Though they'll soon have to*, she said.

We came off the track just before Old Port station.

'The line's live from there,' she explained. 'Because of the navy. Because . . .' She trailed off, but I knew she meant war. 'Anyway,' she carried on. 'It isn't far now.'

'How do you know the way here?' Sam said. 'There's no track.'

She opened her bag and pulled out a big blue book. An olden days thing, its spine broken, its paper torn, but enough of it that I could see the title: *RAC Map of Britain*.

I didn't know what 'RAC' meant but I knew the other words. Map. Like Dad had in the car. But, 'Britain?' I asked. 'That's ages ago. What if it's different? What if . . . if roads have been taken away?'

'Only the names have changed,' she said. 'Back to Old English. John told me. Everything else is the same as it was.'

I can't have looked convinced because she flapped the book open to show me. 'It's got everywhere,' she said. 'All the roads, all the cities. Even yours.'

'Even Brigstowe?' asked Sam.

Poppy nodded. 'Even Brigstowe. Or Bristol, in here. But that's ages away. We've got Plym Mouth to navigate first.' And checking a page with her finger, she looked to both sides, then turned right and started walking. 'Five minutes,' she said.

Five more minutes of walking, then we'd be at the station. Then we'd catch a train and be clattering along the track to Brigstowe – no, Bristol.

Home before we knew it.

So why did my insides feel so slippy?

PLYM MOUTH

It wasn't as big as I'd imagined, but it was busy enough. Eight platforms, all of them with trains waiting or due in, according to the boards. The ticket hall crammed with passengers, some with tickets clamped in their hands, others arguing with guards.

'They've blocked the border,' said Poppy. 'They're not letting anyone across.'

My legs, already unsteady, felt as if they might tremble. 'But what does that mean?'

'For us? Nothing. We're going the other way. But no one can cross to Kernow at all now, papers or not. Only by road up county. Maybe not even that.'

'Because of the war?'

She shrugged. But it didn't look like a casual one. Nothing about her looked casual.

'We should get tickets,' I said then. 'At a machine, though.' I didn't want to talk to anyone who might ask what we were up to – out without an adult, and one of us with home-cut hair who'd turn out to have no papers and be a girl, if they checked. If they searched her. Which I knew they might do.

Maybe that was what was rattling her, or just Albion. I don't know, but I do know that once we'd got the tickets, three of them – not to Brigstowe, but the next stop on, to fool them. Clever, eh? – she suddenly shook her head.

'I can't do it.'

'What?' I held out her ticket, tried to press it into her hand.

She pulled away. 'I can't,' she said. 'I just . . . I can't.'

'Is it the guards?'

She flicked her glance over at them. Milling about in uniform – not train uniform, but military. As if everyone was in the army now.

'Not just them,' she said, turning back. 'It's . . . all of it. I don't like it here. I don't like Albion. I want to go home.'

I thought she was going to sob then but I could hardly hug her, could I? 'But your hair,' I said.

She touched her hand to her scalp as if she'd forgotten. 'It'll grow back.'

I tried again. 'And you've got a ticket.'

'I'm sorry,' she said. 'I've wasted your money.'

'Doesn't matter,' said Sam.

'What?' I frowned at him.

He smiled. 'It's just the Game, isn't it? We'll get it back.'

'I should go,' she said then.

I tried to think of something – anything – to say that might make her stay. But I knew it was useless. And cruel, maybe. Albion was my home, but it wasn't hers.

Instead, I swung my rucksack off and rummaged in it. Pulled something out. 'Here,' I said.

'Your penknife?'

I nodded. 'You'll need it more than me. I only

ever used it at the farm. And' – I felt my face redden
– 'on you.'

'But—'

'You gave me a necklace and I didn't give you
anything. Just take it, will you.'

I wanted her to get it over with, to just go, if she
was going.

She took it. 'I'll look after it,' she said. 'I promise.
And here. You take this.'

It was the *RAC Map of Britain*.

'But Britain doesn't exist any more,' I said.

'Just take it,' she said.

I stuffed it in my rucksack, to make her happy
more than anything because it was just another
heavy thing to lug around.

'Bye,' I said then.

'Bye,' she said back. 'Bye, Sam.'

Sam flung himself at her, held her tight round
her waist, which was all he could reach.

She smiled, a sad, thin sort of smile. 'I'll see you
again, OK? I'll look after the rabbits for you.'

Sam let go then and wouldn't look at her.

Began to fidget again. 'If you like,' he said.

'He'll miss them more than he misses me.' Poppy laughed.

I nodded. 'Me too,' I lied. The biggest lie I'd ever said. Because, yes, I'd miss the rabbits. And the goats and the chickens. And Leon and Minnow. And swimming in the river. And Julia and even Maggie too. Even if she was a villain.

But I'd miss Poppy most of all.

And then I didn't care what anyone thought and I hugged her, so hard I might have squeezed the air out of her. But when I pulled back and looked, it was just tears.

And none of us spoke then.

We just turned our separate ways and began our journeys home.

THE TRAIN

There were ten people in our carriage, scattered about. But we'd grabbed a table, me and Sam, so we could eat our food and read the papers, like you're supposed to on a train.

I'd got them at the Spar at the station. Sam had begged. Not for the papers and comic – that was my idea – but for crisps and biscuits and a can of Coke. The ham sandwich was a compromise. The bread sliced thin, and white as Shirley's fur. Not like the seedy brown chunky doorstops that Maggie and Julia made.

The papers were strange as well. All that news we'd not been allowed for months. Facts crammed into every corner. Or *fakes*, Dad would have said. But I didn't know what was truth any more so I read it anyway. 'Three days to cave!' announced one headline. 'No surrender, says Nigel,' another. Then across the page, 'Back off, Euroscum!'

There was something about curfews too. They'd tightened the night one, started it at six in the evening for anyone under fourteen. But that was OK. I checked my watch. It was only eight in the morning now and how long could it take to get to Brigstowe? Three hours? Four, tops?

'Tickets, please.'

We'd not even set off yet. Maybe this was new, like the curfew. I felt a shiver in me as I pulled the tickets out, and our papers and all. Just in case.

'Where you off to then, son?' asked the guard. He was short and red-faced and had a moustache that sat like a fat caterpillar on his thin lip.

'Glewster,' I said. 'Like on the ticket.'

The guard nodded and I could see a drip of sweat run from his forehead and then off, plop, on to the card. 'And what's at Glewster?'

'Our dad,' I said. Which wasn't a total lie. He worked near there after all and right then, he might have been there.

I could feel Sam fidget and I nudged him to shut up, in case he was thinking of saying anything. But he was busy with his bag, sticking his sandwich in it, not even in the wrapper. I didn't bother telling him off though.

'And where's your mum then?'

'Huh?' I looked back at the guard.

'Isn't she with you?'

'She's . . . pregnant,' I said then. 'Can't travel in case the baby just, you know, pops out.' I don't know why I said it. I knew they didn't just pop out. They strained and ripped and tore through you. But I was flustered and didn't know how else to justify us. 'They're broke up,' I added then, for authenticity. 'We've got two homes. One in Plym Mouth and one in Br— Glewster.'

'Do we?' asked Sam all of a sudden.

'Yes we do.' I kicked at him. He yelped, but I pretended it was nothing. 'We do this all the time,' I carried on. 'This journey, I mean. All by ourselves.'

A woman across from us tutted.

But the guard seem to buy it. Handed back our drippy tickets.

'You know where to change?' he checked.

I nodded. As if I was always doing this journey. As if it wasn't once in a lifetime. We had to change at Brigstowe, didn't we? If we were actually going to Glewster. But we weren't. Brigstowe was it.

Then, satisfied, he moved on down the carriage.

I sucked a big breath in and out and leant back in my seat. But only for a moment.

'Two houses,' came a voice. 'It's not right.'

I looked over. It was the tutting woman with her husband. Both of them thin and rigid and noses wrinkled as if they could smell something yucky. 'Poor little mite,' she added, looking at Sam.

'He doesn't mind,' I said. 'Two Christmases.'

'Jesus isn't real though,' said Sam.

The woman stiffened even more than before. I kicked at Sam again.

'Ow!' he yelped. 'Why d'you keep doing that?'

But I didn't answer, I didn't have time. Because just then the doors beeped and shut with a thunk.

Then a guard on the platform blew a whistle. And then, with a creak and a heave, the train trundled out of the station and along the track through Plym Mouth. Past the grey terraces, past hulking industrial estates, past the very edges where the new houses were, away from the bustle and rough. Where the right people, clean people, could be safe. Though I wondered how Europe would know that, and whether they'd just bomb the lot.

But I couldn't worry about that now. Couldn't worry that our house was in the middle of a city. Right in the bull's eye. Because Dad would have a plan anyway, once we were there. He'd know what to do. He'd make it all normal again.

And with that happy thought clattering loud as the track, I pulled out my own sandwich – my first food since the folly – and began to eat.

ASLEEP

'Tunnel!' yelled Sam.

In a sudden rumble we were plunged into black, the carriage whistling and sucking as we were heaved under the hills, and then, just as sudden, we were thrown out into a deep green valley and into my head came the hymn from school: all about Albion being the New Jerusalem. The Promised Land.

But was it? Was it any better than No Man's Land? Than Caledonia? Than any other place? The countryside wasn't. Or it didn't seem so to me. Same trees, same grass, same hedgerows. The river was different. Here it spread into an estuary, wider and flatter and browner than ours— than Poppy's, I meant. No forest rising up at the sides, instead boatyards and bridges and beach huts.

'The sea!' Sam yelled again and this time he rushed over to the seats on the other side of the carriage, peering over the tutting woman and her huffing husband to get a better look at the flat pancake of blue.

'Do you mind?' snapped the lady.

Sam ignored her. 'Are we driving on water?'

'No, Sam.' I pulled him back. 'Just the edge of it.'

'I thought you did this all the time?' The lady was staring at me.

I felt hot, panicky. 'We do, it's just . . . he's usually asleep.'

'No, I'm not.' Sam was still trying to see out the window. 'Where's over there?' he asked, pointing across the water.

I looked into the distance, where the sea met the sky. 'Europe,' I said quietly, hoping the couple wouldn't hear.

We'd been once, I remembered. To France, I think – a day trip. Sam in Mum's belly by then, Dad driving a different car then – a yellow one, 'held together with gaffer tape and faith' Dad said. Like he said about all his cars. There was bread as well – better than ours:

crisp and delicious. And a dead jellyfish on the sand. And when we stood on the beach, Dad said you could see England on a good day.

Today all we could see was water.

Today was not a good day.

Eventually the train rounded a corner and the sea disappeared. And then it was just fields as far as the eye could see. Sam sat back down properly then and started on the comic I'd got him. And I leant against the window and closed my eyes. I wasn't going to sleep. I was just resting for a minute, thinking of Poppy, hoping she was OK. Hoping she'd got back and Julia hadn't flipped about her hair. Hadn't flipped that we were missing. But that thought sent a whoosh of worry through me so I went back to just Poppy: her rowing us up river; her swimming – the silver of her hair like a mermaid's; her giving me the bead. I touched the necklace then, twisted it in my fingers, wondered what Ahmed would say. What Jayden Nesbitt would say.

And all the while, the train clackety-clacked on.

AWAKE

The tannoy woke me, a woman's voice telling us the next stop was Sarum.

I sat up, embarrassed: my mouth had been wide open and a trickle of dribble was making its way down my chin. And what if I'd snored? I went to ask Sam but he was under the table with something and when I glanced over at the other seats the tutting woman and man were gone. In their place was another old lady, but this one was smiling and fiddling with some knitting.

I smiled at her, quick and neat. She smiled back.

'Nice of them to let him bring his friend on board,' she said.

'Huh?' I said, no idea what she was on about.

'Your little brother.' She nodded at the floor.

'He is your brother, isn't he?'

'Yes, but—'

Something inside me slipped and sent my stomach jumping. Slowly I leant over and peered under the table. It was worse than I'd imagined. He'd not made a friend on the train – started talking to some boy and told him our story, got us into bother or worse, trouble.

No. There was Sam, happy as anything. Because in his lap was a rabbit.

Not a toy one, stuffed. But a real live rabbit with mottled fur and twitching whiskers and a scut of a tail like cotton wool. And not just any random rabbit either – not that you could get a random rabbit on a train – this one, I was pretty sure, was Dave.

'What the flaming hell have you done?' I snapped at him.

'What? You can bring dogs.'

'That's not a dog. It's a rabbit. You can't bring a rabbit on a train, I told you.'

'No you never. You said I couldn't bring a *bunch* of rabbits. This isn't a bunch, it's one.'

'But . . .' It was true, I had said that. But it didn't make what he'd done right. 'If the guard catches you, he'll have it,' I hissed. 'Just put it away for now. We'll let it loose at Brigstowe or something.'

'No!' Sam wailed. 'You can't let him loose!'

'OK, OK,' I tried to calm him. 'But I'm telling you now, Dad's not going to be happy about a rabbit.'

Dad wasn't going to be happy at all, probably. But I couldn't think about that now. I had rabbits to deal with. And how we were going to get from Brigstowe Central back to the house. Because the station was in the middle of the city and we lived on the edge and I didn't know which bus to get or even how to walk.

Only, then I thought of something else. Something worse than a rabbit in a bag: the tannoy lady. She'd said Sarum was the next stop, but Sarum wasn't on the route. I'd looked on the board at Plym Mouth and it was Escanceaster, Twyverton, Tonebridge. Then Brigstowe and something about Readford. No Sarum. And Sarum wasn't anywhere near Brigstowe; it was further down and past it, practically in Londinium.

'Excuse me,' I said to the lady. 'Do you know where this train's going?'

She looked up from the clacking of needles. 'Sarum, then Readford, then Londinium,' she said.

I felt dizzy then, and sick. I'd messed up. I'd fallen asleep and somehow, we'd ended up on the wrong train.

'What about Brigstowe?' I said.

'Brigstowe?' she repeated. 'You had to change at Tonebridge for that. Didn't you check?'

'Yes— No, I . . .' I remembered the conductor suddenly and my stomach plummeted. I really had messed up. I hadn't done what Dad had said. I may have been brave but I hadn't been clever, I hadn't looked out for Sam. Because here we were on the wrong train, with a rabbit. My eyes prickled with tears and a lump stuck in my throat. 'How . . . how do we get to Brigstowe from here?' I managed.

She smiled. 'Oh, love.' She fumbled in her pocket and pulled out a hankie. 'Here.' She handed it to me and I took it, wiped at my face quick so Sam, who was back in his seat, wouldn't see. 'You'll need to change at Readford, get a train back from there to Brigstowe Parkway.'

'Not Brigstowe Central?'

'That's shut,' she said.

My insides stuttered again. Brigstowe Parkway was miles away. Outside the city to the north and we lived south.

'Blame the Resistance,' she said, spitting out the word like a pip.

'What do you mean?'

'Bomb threats. To scupper the war. Flaming loons, 'scuse my language. Sooner Albion gets them sorted the better, if you ask me.' She jabbed at the air with her knitting. 'Them and the foreigners they're so fond of.'

She was an Albioneer? So why was she being nice? Though I suppose even Nice Nana hadn't been too fond of 'foreigners'. Didn't like the food. Though she liked it enough to move to Spain.

'You'll be fine,' she said then. 'Won't even need a new ticket, I expect. Though you may have to wait a while for a train. There's stoppages up Londinium way. Strikes, I've heard.'

'Because of the war?'

She nodded. 'Probably more Resistance. You'd think they'd be more patriotic, wouldn't you? Albion's hour of need. Suppose we're lucky this one's running.'

I nodded. Took a breath and held it to steady myself. We'd be fine. She'd said so, hadn't she? And even if we had to wait, we'd still be home before curfew.

Sam leant on me and sighed, clutching his snuffling bag to him. 'Are we nearly there yet?' he asked.

'Nearly,' I lied. 'Nearly.'

THE WALK

'I'm tired,' complained Sam.

'You said that ten minutes ago,' I snapped. 'I'm tired too, but there's nothing I can do.' There wasn't. It was four before we'd got a train from Readford. That got us in just gone five, which meant we only had an hour before curfew. Least I had the map so I knew which way to go. Poppy was right, the roads were all still there, just the names had changed. Like our road used to be Mandela Street but now it was Bentley. I wondered who had changed them. Albion, I guessed. But why?

'I'm hungry,' said Sam, trying a different tactic.

'We'll eat when we get in,' I said. 'There'll be food in the fridge.'

I didn't know if that was true any more than

I knew if Dad would be in when we got there, and what he'd have to say. Perhaps he was an Albioneer and all, he'd just hidden it. Or Resistance even.

I didn't know the answers. I just knew we had to get back.

But by five to six we were still more than two miles away. Still skirting the edge of the city, the river and bridge dropping down to the right, the downs to our left. And us in the middle of another wood. In the middle of nowhere.

'Why've we stopped?' asked Sam.

'Because we have to,' I said. 'We've got to stop here for the night.'

Sam looked around. 'Where? Where's the beds?'

'Here.' I nodded at the ground, bumpy and tufted.

'But—'

'Just don't,' I blurted. Then, quick, wiping my tears away along with my snot, 'I'm sorry. I just . . . we don't have enough time. If we stay out and someone catches us, then . . .'

'We'd be in prison,' he said. 'Until someone freed us. Or we won enough points.'

'What?'

'In the Game,' he said.

I laughed, and a bogey flew out of my nose on to the floor, which made Sam laugh. 'Yes,' I said. 'In the Game.'

'What's my special power?' he asked then. 'Can I have jet throwers?'

'You can have whatever you like. Even invisibility. Even fingers that shoot out mince.'

Sam grinned. 'Mince fingers.'

'I'll be able to melt anything,' I said. 'Even stone.'

And on we went, making up powers until the sun dipped behind the hills in the distance and the heat disappeared, and our laughter with it.

**

I couldn't get the flint to work, not like Poppy and Leon.

'Should've got matches,' said Sam.

'Matches is cheating,' I snapped back at him. And I struck the keys again but even when I managed to make a spark it wouldn't take to the paper. Probably because Sam had spilt juice on it, which I told him.

'Why's it my fault?' he said. 'It's always my fault.'

'Because it is your fault. You spilt the juice. You brought the stupid rabbit so now we don't even have sandwiches.'

'He's not stupid and he was hungry,' wailed Sam.

I stormed off then. I didn't know where I was going. Not far, but far enough to get away from my brother for a bit. Far enough to forgive him.

Far enough that he had time to get my phone where I'd shoved it in the rucksack.

'What are you doing?' I asked, my heart speeding up, fast as a mouse's now.

'Texting Dad.'

'What?'

'Look!' he held it up. 'I did a text!'

I snatched it, and felt my heart thunk and shudder. He had texted. But not in code. Not clever. In actual words. Hello Dad, it said. Weer comming to see you.

'You idiot,' I said. 'You actual idiot.'

'Shut up!' wailed Sam. 'You're not allowed to call me that. I'm telling!' And he tried to grab the phone back off me.

And then, I don't know why, who I was protecting, but I did something worse, even less clever: I threw it. I pulled my arm back and I hurled the phone into the darkness.

Neither of us said anything for a moment.

We just stood, me feeling stupid, Sam feeling I don't know what, staring into the gloom.

'Shall we fetch it?' Sam said eventually.

'Yes,' I said. 'We probably should.'

***

But we didn't. We couldn't. It was too dark and too vast and there were things in the wood, noises. And in the end we gave up.

'I'll look in the morning,' I said.

Sam nodded, and went back to his rabbit: grey nose snuffling, the twilight eyes currant-black and bright. And I remembered Harry Potter then, eyes milky as Mr Minton's, nailed to the door.

'Be careful of him,' I said. 'I mean, watch he

doesn't get loose.'

'He won't,' said Sam, handing him a snatch of grass then lying on his side, curled in a comma, the bag safe against his belly. 'Tell me a story,' he said then.

'A story?'

He nodded. 'A bedtime story. Like Dad does.'

'I don't know any.'

'Oh.'

I lay down, my own head propped on my bag, turned on to my side. Something in my pocket crackled.

'There is something,' I said. 'Not a story but . . . well, maybe it is.'

'Is it true?' Sam asked.

'Every word.'

And I read him the List then, but with added adventure. With peril. With a princess – Mum, of course – and an almost-handsome prince, who doesn't quite rescue her. I told him about the colour of her hair – reddish like conkers. The smell of her – lemons. The song she sung about heroes, which I tried to sing a bit, but couldn't remember the words. I told him everything I remembered: her best tea, boarding school, even the bunker.

'There's a bunker under our house?' he said, incredulous. 'No way.'

'Yes way,' I said. 'But you're not to go in it.'

'Not 'til I'm big?'

'Not ever.'

'We'll see,' said Sam.

And I didn't bother to argue. Because right then, he was happy. With his story and his rabbit and his dad in the morning. Because it was all a game. Just a game, to him.

But I knew better. I knew the truth. And the truth was we didn't know what tomorrow held.

No one did.

BENTLEY STREET
(five days after D-Day,
two days before war)

The first thing that went wrong was Dave. Because when we woke up, he was gone.

'I don't understand,' said Sam. 'I told him not to go anywhere.'

'And rabbits speak English, do they?'

'It's your fault,' he wailed. 'You're oldest.'

'I didn't even want to bring him!' I yelled.

'Because you're mean!' snapped Sam. 'And horrible. And I hate you!'

'Like I care!'

Only I did. And not just because Dad had told me to. 'Look,' I said. 'He's a rabbit. He's used to . . .' – I flapped my hands at the ground around me –

'this. It's how rabbits are meant to live. How they all used to live.'

Sam's voice was jumpy and huffling. 'But he's on his own.'

I shook my head. 'He'll have found friends. Rabbit friends.'

Sam wiped snot on his sleeve. 'Do you think?'

'I know.'

Sam thought for a moment. Then he said, 'I need a poo.'

'Can't you wait? We'll be home in an hour or so.'

But he couldn't. He had to go. Which meant he had to go on the ground.

That was the second thing to go wrong because we didn't have any paper, only comic, and that was shiny and didn't wipe properly and then he got poo on his pants and had to take them off and they were his best Spider-Man ones.

'You'll just have to leave them,' I said.

'No,' said Sam. 'Dad'll wash them.'

'I'm not carrying your stinking pants,' I said.

'You should've got paper then,' said Sam.

In the end Sam carried them. Wrapped in his jumper, which would need a wash as well. Everything would, including us – we must've stunk as bad as the pants. But we could shower, soon as we got in. That's what I kept telling myself. Shower and have breakfast and then sit in the living room and tell Dad all about it and then go back to Normal.

Only that's not what was going to happen, was it. And I think I knew it even then.

**

I pressed the bell, heard the tinkle of it down the hallway. But then it was silent. There was no sign of life. No sound from the house at all. Not even the clunk of someone lumbering about.

'Have you got a key?' said Sam.

'Yeah, 'cause I've carried that about with me.'

'You might have.'

'Well, I haven't.' And there wasn't a spare either, Dad always said it was too risky.

'You could smash it in,' said Sam. 'Or melt it.'

But we didn't have melting powers, or flame-shooting fingers and 'open sesame' was just a story and all. And I couldn't break in, even if I was strong enough, because I had to be careful, didn't I, with Paris just next door, ears wigging and nose ready to beak into our business.

I sighed and leant my forehead against the door. And for a second I thought I was fainting, because the world seemed to tip and teeter. Only, it wasn't the world shifting. It was me. The door was wide open and I was falling through it.

I staggered up from the mat, shut the door behind us quick, Sam laughing like it's all some massive joke. Some massive game. 'Shut up,' I snapped. Because this wasn't funny. Not just me falling, but the door.

Because it wasn't just on the latch, left ready for us in case we came calling, or 'cause Dad had popped over the road or into the garage for a minute. It was smashed in, the lock gone, the surround splintered.

'Who do you think done it?' asked Sam. 'Villains?'

My heart was mouse-fast again, my throat tight. 'Maybe,' I said.

'Do you think they're still here?'

I put a hand on Sam's mouth to shush him,

listened hard, but there was nothing, just the hum of the fridge. I shook my head. 'Gone,' I said, but I whispered it. In case.

'Can I have breakfast, then?' Sam whispered back.

I didn't know how he could even think about food. I knew I'd be sick if I tried. But I led him into the kitchen all the same.

The first thing I noticed was the smell.

There was still the home smell – the musty coffee pot, the lemon of laundry, the herby pot on the window sill. But there was something stale as well. Like bread gone mouldy, or washing that's stayed damp for days 'cause no one's bothered to hang it.

Sam yanked open the fridge, grabbed the milk.

'Wait!' I hissed before he drank it down. I sniffed it and sick rose in me. It was yoghurty and off so I tipped it in the sink, swilled it out. 'You'll have to have water,' I whispered.

'On cereal? You can't have water on cereal. That's like . . . breaking the law or something.'

'It isn't,' I insisted. 'Just do it. Please.' I wanted him to shut up so I could think.

Sam clattered a bowl down from the cupboard and, finger on my lips, I hushed him again. Then, exaggerated, he quietly poured Cheerios into it, topped it up with water from the tap. Least it wouldn't kill him.

'Where's Dad then?' he whispered, his mouth full of watery clag. 'Is he with them? Have they kidnapped him? Is there a ransom?'

'God, Sam!' I snapped then, remembering myself. 'I just . . . I don't know.'

I could feel tears well again, feel my face hot and my limbs jitter. This wasn't what was supposed to happen. This couldn't be happening. I scanned the room, frantic, looking for something – anything. Then I sped round the house to see if anything was missing, if Dad had packed. But his suitcase was still under his bed, his clothes still hanging or stacked, and some scattered – but that was normal, wasn't it? Floor wardrobe, he called it.

I traipsed back to the kitchen with a big fat nothing and a hollowness inside. 'I don't know, Sam,' I said. 'I don't—'

But then I saw it, on the fridge. The magnets —
the letters that spelled out 'Sam smells' and 'Alan
is best'. They didn't spell that any more. They didn't
spell anything that looked like normal words.
Instead they said '**JO UIF CVOLFS**'.

JO UIF CVOLFS.

My insides jinked and skittered. I knew this.
I could do it.

I counted back a letter from each one, found the
right magnet, clacked it on to the fridge in front
of me until I had it: a gem of a sentence that made
absolute sense.

'IN . . . THE . . . BUN . . . BUN—'

'Bunker,' I finished for him.

'Bunker?' said Sam. 'I thought we weren't allowed
in there. I thought it was shut.'

'It was,' I said.

It was. Until something changed. Until war came
knocking. Because then someone had needed to hide.
Someone had opened it. Someone was down there.
And I was pretty sure I knew who that someone was.

DAD

I should've noticed when we came in – the rug on the kitchen floor had shifted, was rucked up at one end. I flapped it back and felt a flicker of brilliance along with the sickness, because there it was, a trapdoor, like something out of *Scooby Doo*. Just sitting there in our kitchen, under our feet all those times we ate Cheerios and drank chocolate milk and argued about who would win in a fight: Thor or a T-rex.

'Oh. My. GOD!' said Sam, who was practically prancing now, hopping about, his bowl still in his hand, spilling cereal over the floorboards.

'Stop,' I said. 'This is serious.'

And it was. Deadly serious. The most serious thing I'd ever dealt with – even more than Noah's tattoo. Even more than the dead rabbit. Or the missing one.

The metal ring was still there, sunk into one side of it, cold to the touch and rusty. I clasped it, took a breath and pulled. It lifted with a whump of air that sent dust up our noses and on to our clothes. Coughing and flapping, we waited until it had stopped and then peered into the black. Saw the rungs of a ladder leading down into nothingness – a black hole; a void.

Void or not, I had to go down, I knew it. Though none of me wanted to. I just wanted someone to come and make it all right. A hero – or heroine. Julia or Poppy or Maggie even.

Or Dad.

But Dad was why I had to do this. Dad hadn't come to rescue me. I had to rescue him.

So, step by creaking step, I lowered myself down.

'Can I come? I want to come!'

'Just a minute,' I said. 'Wait.'

Seven steps then at the bottom I turned and tried to focus, let the blurs take shape. There were shelves, stacked with tins of things and bottled water – I remembered those, I thought, from before. A bucket or something small and squat. And there was a sofa too – fat and padded and waiting, like all of this was. Waiting for war. But war had come, or would in two days.

That was when I heard it, in the dark and the fust. Something shuffling, an animal sound. It smelt of animal too – sweat and pee and worse. Not like Dad at all. Had I messed up? Was this a trap?

Dizzy sickness swirled in me and sent my legs trembling, my heart pat-pat-pattering like the tap of a tiny hammer. 'Is . . . is something there?' *God, what an idiot*, I thought soon as I'd said it. Like a 'thing' would answer. A fox or a dog or even a villain.

But something did answer. Something whimpered, and then, in a voice like cracking paint, said my name.

'Alan?'

And in that word the world exploded and came back again in a wondrous rush. Sam with it, scuttling spider-like down the ladder and across to me.

And we stood there, the pair of us, looking into

the gloom. Then I remembered my torch, pulled it out of my pocket, picked out the shelves, the bucket, the sofa in its weak beam. And there it— he was. Crouched in a corner, hunched and hugging himself.

'Dad!' I flung myself at him, hurled myself on to his legs and worked my way into his arms, my head in his chest. Felt him take me, weakly, smelt the stink of his pits, and his pee and all.

Sam was next, scuttling down the steps then burrowing in like a bunny until he was nestled in, smell and all. 'You honk,' he said.

'I know,' said Dad.

He reached up and I knew what he was doing – wiping tears. And my heart hurt then, because I'd not seen him do that since Mum.

'What happened?' I asked.

'Were there villains?' asked Sam.

'Don't be stupid.' I shoved him.

'Hey,' said Dad, his voice still brittle.

'But were there?' repeated Sam.

I waited for Dad to explain – the mistake,

the mess up. That he'd forgot his key, dropped it, got stuck somehow, trapped down here.

But then he said it. The truth.

'Yes,' he said. 'There were.'

***

He told us what then, and who: Albioneers had come to fetch him, a whole bunch of them. He'd heard the van, heard them assemble with weapons, heard them hollering at the door. But he'd been ready for them, he said. 'Cause he'd known it would happen. Known he didn't have time to run. But he had enough time to hide. That's when he left the message on the fridge.

'When?' I said.

'A week ago. Maybe more. I don't know exactly.'

'That's when you stopped texting.'

He nodded.

'But why didn't you bring your phone down?' asked Sam.

'I didn't think of everything,' he said. 'Didn't think of a tin-opener either.'

'Have you not eaten?' I asked. 'In a week?'

'I had some crackers,' he said. 'And some gum.'

Crackers and gum. And we'd moaned about only a sandwich.

'What's that?' asked Sam, kicking at the bucket.

I heard a slopping sound as Dad grabbed him, said, 'Don't touch that!'

It was the toilet, had to be. I tried not to think of my own dad squatting on a bucket. Worse than Sam in the woods. My face reddened with his shame.

'Why didn't you just go upstairs?' I said.

'I was scared they'd be waiting.'

'The Albioneers?' I asked.

Dad nodded.

'But *why* did they come for you?' Sam said. 'Are *you* the villain?'

Dad shook his head. 'Because I quit my job. And they knew I—' But he stopped himself.

'Knew what?' I asked. 'Are you Resistance? You are, aren't you.' Sick was in me again, slopping about, and I didn't know if it was good sick, like on a rollercoaster, or bad.

'Not . . . not how you think.'

'Not the ones with guns?'

'No guns,' said Dad. 'Least, only Maggie I think. And that's only for the animals.'

Maggie! So he was in on it, in on everything! But—

Then I remembered it. What Maggie had said. That there were different ways to resist. And I wondered what they were doing. And who was doing it, exactly.

'Who else?' I asked.

'Me and Ringo,' Dad said. 'Maggie. Julia. John, too.'

'But he comes into Albion,' I said. 'He gets marshmallows and stuff.'

'And runs messages. And spreads the word for the women.'

My heart was pounding now, eager for it. 'What word?'

'Where to come. When it's time.'

'Time for what?'

'To leave Albion and head for—'

'No Man's Land!' I blurted, getting it now.

'No Man's Land.'

I saw them then. The women in the kitchen, whispering, drinking, planning. Not bad things. But not nothing either. Providing a new life for anyone who needed it.

They weren't nobodies.

They were heroes after all.

'So you've been down here the whole time?' I asked then.

Dad nodded.

'But you can come out now,' said Sam. 'The Game's over. We've saved you!'

Dad laughed, a split, difficult thing that I knew hid more tears. 'Sam,' he said, and hugged us tighter. 'It's only just starting.'

That's when I got it. That this wasn't the end. There was no celebration, no heroes' return. We'd just left safety and walked straight into the fire.

HELP

'I could get the phone,' I said. 'Then we could call someone.'

'Who?' asked Sam.

'Julia,' I said.

Dad shook his head. 'You can't go up. It's too risky.'

'So what?' I asked. 'We just wait here and hope Spider-Man smashes in and rescues us? Or Wolverine? Or Hulk?'

'Hulk would be good,' said Sam. 'He could break everything.'

'Why would that be good?' I asked. 'Just shut up if you can't be helpful.'

'Boys,' said Dad. 'There's no need—'

'Yes there is!' I blurted. 'You said to be brave.

You said to be clever. Then everything would go back to normal. Well, it hasn't. What's normal about living in a cellar with beans we can't even eat? Being brave is going upstairs. Being clever is getting the phone and calling Julia. Then she can fetch us. Then we can go back . . .' But I couldn't say it. Couldn't admit that No Man's Land was home. Was where we were supposed to be.

'Alan,' said Dad, trying to hug me, but I wriggled out of his grasp and stood.

'We can't stay here,' I said. 'We've got to do something.'

And I said it like I meant it, looked at him hard, like a hero would. Even though inside I felt weak, felt as flimsy as river reeds. *But it was like smiling*, I thought. You had to fake it until you make it. So I stood strong as Superman. And I was expecting Dad to stop me, to say, 'No, Alan, don't.' But maybe he was too weak himself. Maybe he knew I was right. Whichever, in the end he nodded.

'Go on then,' he said. 'It's in my coat pocket. Charger's in the kitchen. But be quick.'

***

I was quick. Quicker then I'd ever been on sports day or racing in the park. I shot up the ladder and into the kitchen, yanked the charger out of the wall and scrambled the letters on the fridge, then headed into the hall. I stuck my hand into one pocket. Nothing. Then the other – felt the metal and glass of it, cold and oblong. Pulled it out and was about to spin back when I heard my name again.

'Alan?'

I started. This wasn't Dad or Sam. This was a girl. And it wasn't coming from the bunker, it was coming from the other side of the front door.

'Alan,' she said again. 'I know you're in there. I can hear you.'

Paris.

I didn't move a muscle. Not a twitch or a flicker. But the door creaked and heaved and then there she was anyway, staring at me, mouth open.

'I knew it was you,' she said. 'I knew you'd come back.'

'I . . .'

'Everyone's gone,' she said.

'Everyone?'

'Pretty much.'

'Even Ahmed?'

She nodded.

I felt sick. 'Gone where?'

'Somewhere outside Glasgu.'

So he was safe then, at least.

'I thought you were going to the Forest of Dene?' I said then.

Something happened to Paris then. She seemed to shrink into herself. 'My dad said no. He said . . .' She was struggling for words. 'He said we had to stay and be brave and Albion would save us.'

Pity swilled in me. Even though she'd been mean. Even though I was no better off than her. But then, she wasn't better off than me either. Not any more. 'Maybe they will,' I said.

But Paris just shrugged. 'Where were you?' she said then.

'Somewhere . . . safe.'

'Then why did you come back?'

'Just – we forgot something.'

'And now you're going back.'

I nodded slowly.

'I want to come,' said Paris suddenly. 'Please let me come.'

'But—'

'Please!' she begged.

'Paris?'

I jumped. The voice came from outside. Close.

'You mustn't tell,' I begged.

But something had switched, flicked back. She stared at me, hardness in her eyes again. 'My dad says your dad is Resistance. They're looking for him, you know. And they'll find him. Unless . . . unless you take me.'

'But I can't,' I said. 'I don't—'

'Then I'll tell. Right now, I'll tell.'

'Paris!' came the voice again.

'OK!' I scrabbled for something to offer her. 'Tomorrow,' I said. 'Come back tomorrow and I'll take you.'

'Take me to safety?'

I nodded.

'War starts in two days.'

'I know,' I said.

'You'd better not be lying.'

'I'm not.'

Paris nodded, swallowing it. 'Tomorrow then,' she said.

'Tomorrow.'

'Paris? You in there?'

'Go on then,' she hissed.

I didn't wait to be told twice. I charged the other way, down the hall, across the kitchen – grabbing the box of Cheerios, an apple, a black banana – then clambering down again into the bunker, pulling the trapdoor over me so the only light left was the weak beam of my torch.

'Thank God,' said Dad. 'I thought something . . . I thought—'

'Shhhh!' I urged.

And he did. And so did Sam.

And we heard it then.

The thud of feet coming down the hall.

The banging of doors being flung wide to find us.

The voice of Paris, standing on the rug right above our heads – she must've shuffled it back herself – muffled, but enough to make out what she was saying.

'They're not here,' she insisted. 'I told you, didn't I?'

'What was you even doing in here?' her dad said back. 'Stupid bloody girl. Stupid as your mother.'

I heard a smack then. And a sound from Paris's mouth like Leon's groan, only higher.

And it was as if my own stomach had been punched or my own head had been slapped. Because it should have been. She'd taken that for me. She didn't have to. She could have told the truth but she kept our secret.

And she carried on keeping it and all.

'I promise,' she sobbed. 'I haven't seen them.'

Her dad snorted then. 'Probably run off, en't they. Cowards. That's all they are. Bunch of bloody girls.'

'Yeah,' said Paris. 'Bloody girls.'

I heard a shift then. Feet clomping off. The slam

of a door that wouldn't shut, banging back and forth on its hinges.

And I said a silent thank you to all those bloody girls who were trying to save us. Julia and Maggie and Poppy.

And Paris too.

Then I handed Sam the cereal, handed Dad the phone and the charger. He plugged it in, waited for the ting of the battery back into life, then tapped a message out quickly. I didn't need to ask who to.

'Now what?' I asked.

'Now we wait.'

THE DISCOVERY
(the day before war)

I don't know how long we waited. The torch went and the phone glow only lit up our faces, blue and spooky. And down there, time seemed like a piece of elastic, all stretched out and strange so that minutes could have been hours and hours days, but a day might've been a minute as well.

We played who would win in a fight. Played rock, paper, scissors, even letting Sam have 'lightsaber' (which beats everything). Even tried I-Spy, only that didn't work because it was hard to see and even when you could, there wasn't much to look at and Sam kept picking 'p' for poo and Dad was embarrassed. We all were. Until we needed to go – then we were just glad.

And through all of it, we were sick and tired and

scared and desperate. Because what if this was it? What if nobody came? Or what if the wrong people did and took us away? We'd all heard what they did to Traitors, and prison was the best of it. The kids they'd take to warehouses, make them sleep in cages, not even letting them stay with relatives in case they were Traitors too.

'Don't be a hero,' Dad had said.

But I was glad I'd tried. Because at least we were together. And I wished then that Noah was with me. Could have borrowed my dad instead of trying to find his, like I'd borrowed his mum.

And then I remembered it: 'If wishes were horses, beggars would ride.'

Mum said it.

Another thing for my list. And I held them in my head like gems then, all sixteen of them.

And minutes tick-tocked on.

***

Sam and Dad were asleep when I heard it. The creak of the front door, the steps in the hallway, the mutters and muffled hushing that all came to a halt above our heads.

I nudged Dad awake, held a finger to my lips in the glow of the phone so he could see, then pointed it up at the trapdoor.

Dad nodded, and we stared at each other then, saying everything and nothing with just our eyes: I hate this, I love you, I'm sorry. Then we held hands round Sam, who was snuffling asleep still, and squeezed tight, so tight my fingers clicked.

This was it. This was do or die. This was the moment Batman would be dragged from the Lazarus Pit to meet his fate. And whether he would win or lose would depend on who he had to fight.

I held my breath as I heard someone grunt, kick back the rug. Was that Mr Metcalfe? Or was it too soft?

Then the trapdoor lifted and sunlight spilt in so we had to squint even as we held our breath. But when I saw who it was, I let out a gasp.

Hair, tufted and stubbly. Skinny limbs strong from swimming and conker-brown from the sun. An elder bead on a nettle necklace, its single letter standing for her name.

P.

For Poppy.

BACK TO KERNOW

We took nothing with us. There wasn't time. And John said whatever we needed, if Julia or Maggie didn't have it, he'd be able to get it for us, somehow.

No one talked much on the journey back in his van. We couldn't, crouched as we were in crates or slipped inside sacks, pretending we were nothing but bags of potatoes, boxes of veg. Praying it wouldn't come to them checking. That we'd slip unnoticed into the night like Dad had that time, lights out, engine off as we slid down the hill to the water.

John took a different road, up across the moor then off road, jerking us about so my elbows banged the van and someone was sick; I could tell by the smell. Sam, I reckoned. But he didn't even cry this time.

He was too scared for that.

We all were.

But somehow, somehow, without special powers or capes or even guns, we made it.

***

Light was blooming by the time we got to Kernow, shafts of it shimmering on the roofs of Tamar, of Julia's house, of the barn and the rabbit hutches and, up in the woods – though I couldn't see it – on the Folly and all. And the farm was busy, the day already started. Minnow dancing round us; Leon on the wall, legs dangling and banging; Maggie clattering around with her own business.

Not clattering around too much for a hug. I threw myself at her. So hard she grunted. But I could tell it wasn't a cross noise. Just a surprised one.

'Came back, did you?' she said.

I didn't say anything. Just held on tight, drinking in the old-lady smell of her. Saying a massive 'thank you' in my head.

'So this is it,' Dad said, when I'd let go. 'Best show me where we're sleeping.'

'Mine for now,' said Maggie. ''Til we get the tents sorted.'

'Tents?'

'What do you think we've been up to for months?' Julia said. 'Nothing?'

My face felt red as my wellies. 'No,' I said. 'I just . . .'

'It's fine.' She smiled. 'We should have told you.'

'I'll show you,' added Poppy, her hand skimming mine. 'If you like.'

And I did like. I liked all of it. I liked being here, I realised. With these women. These nobodies that Albion'd have down as a waste of space. But something else was pressing. Something I wanted Dad to see. To show him what I could do.

'Later,' I said. Then I looked at Julia and grinned. 'But first, work.'

***

Leaning into Shirley was like leaning into another jumpery, womany hug – warm and soft and fusty. And the milk came quick, the squirts turning from clink to splish in minutes until the tin bucket was full.

'See,' I said, eager to show him as Sam had been when he'd shown Dad the rabbits.

Dad was smiling. Wide, so wide. 'You know your mum loved that,' he said. 'Milking the goats.'

My heart flickered. 'She did?'

'She did. Could never get the hang of it myself though.'

'You will,' I said. And I smiled too, to match him. 'You'll have to.'

'Then you can teach me,' he said. 'With that big loaf of yours.'

And I knew he didn't mean bread then. It was code. Loaf of bread meant 'head'. He was saying I was brainy.

We all were, I reckoned, in No Man's Land. Men and women and kids.

And that was as good as being heroes any day.

HOME

(a hundred days after war)

The worst bit is Paris. Because I'd broken my promise to fetch her. Because John said we couldn't, not now. And I knew he was right. But it wasn't her fault, being an Albioneer. She wasn't a villain, not really. It was only what her parents taught her. Same as Noah and his dad.

He never came back; no one's heard from him since that day of the rabbit. But Poppy says he'll come one day, she's sure of it.

And so every day we look for them – Paris and Noah and Laura and all – in the slow stream of people that arrive, fat with hope, drawn from all over. And they're all kinds of people – white and black and gay and straight, and some twisted, some hunched, some shuffling, but all the same really. All of them refugees, all of them following John's word, risking their lives to cross the Tamar, that channel of water that separates Albion from No Man's Land. Because all of them believe, like we do, that we're better together.

I don't know if the world will go back to how it was before war, before Albion even. I don't know if I'll see Ahmed again or Mrs King or anyone from then.

But if we don't, then it wouldn't be the end of the world.

Because that's just it. War is still raging – we can hear the guns sometimes, over in Plym Mouth: Albion firing at Europe over the water; them firing back – but the world is still going. It's coping, somehow. We just had to learn to think differently. To accept that being a hero doesn't mean raising your weapon, beating an enemy, claiming victory. Sometimes it just means finding a new way to live.

That normal is what you want it to be.
That home is wherever you make it.
And this, now, is home.

ALAN'S CAESAR SHIFT

A	B	C	D	E	F	G	H	I	J	K	L	M
B	C	D	E	F	G	H	I	J	K	L	M	N

N	O	P	Q	R	S	T	U	V	W	X	Y	Z
O	P	Q	R	S	T	U	V	W	X	Y	Z	A

Acknowledgements

With thanks to my agent Julia Churchill, my editor Emma Roberts and all at UCLan, my friends Mark Taylor-Batty, for letting me borrow some of the brilliant things his boys have said, and Helen Stringfellow, for teaching me to build a fire and make nettle thread, Millie, for keeping me laughing through lockdown, the real Poppy and Noah whose names and faces I shamelessly borrowed as I wrote, my students and former colleagues on the MA in Writing for Young People at Bath Spa – hope hunters, all – and to Rik, for listening.

IF YOU LIKE THIS, YOU'LL LOVE . . .

What if you could conjure the clouds?

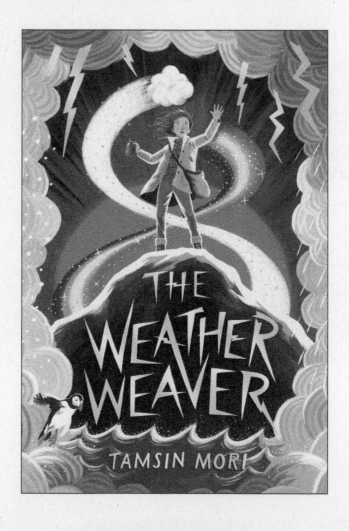

The Secret Library Service: Who Reads Wins!

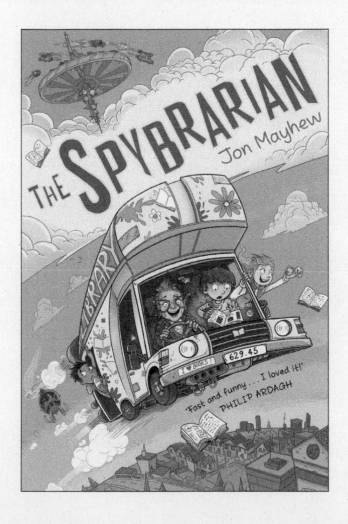

Lace up your boots and get ready for kick off –
Try this fantastic fiction series inspired by the
trailblazers of Women's football.

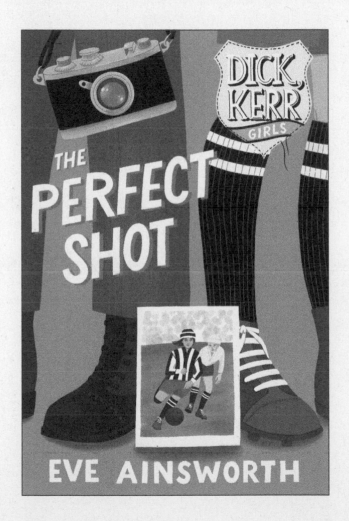

DICK, KERR GIRLS

THE
PERFECT
SHOT

EVE AINSWORTH

'Satisfyingly sprinkled with clues to sniff out,
this is a timeless, accessible and well-paced
mystery with bags of atmosphere.'
BookTrust

Illustrated by Jenny Czerwonka

Susan Brownrigg

Gracie
Fairshaw
and the
Mysterious
Guest

"DELIGHTFULLY ENGAGING MYSTERY." KATHERINE WOODFINE

Ahoy there! The Nine Sails is casting off
for Madagascar so all aboard for
a treasure hunt you'll never forget!

The first book in a new electrifying series
from the author of *Sky Thieves*, Dan Walker.

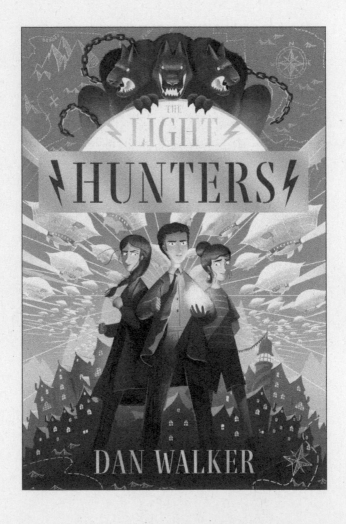

A rollicking medieval romp where laughter
and action abound in equal measure . . .
And where danger lurks around every corner.

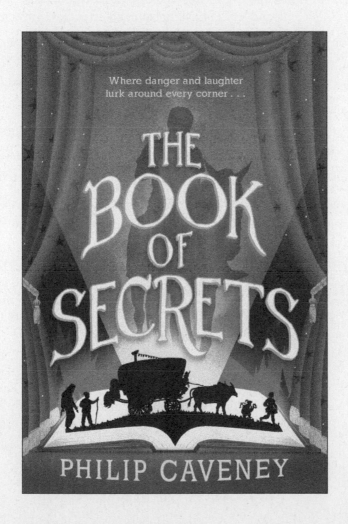

Where danger and laughter
lurk around every corner . . .

THE
BOOK
OF
SECRETS

PHILIP CAVENEY

HAVE YOU EVER WONDERED HOW BOOKS ARE MADE?

UCLan Publishing are based in the North of England and involve BA Publishing and MA Publishing students from the University of Central Lancashire at every stage of the publishing process.

BA Publishing and MA Publishing students are based within our company and work on producing books as part of their course – some of which are selected to be published and printed by UCLan Publishing. Students also gain first-hand experience of negotiating with buyers, conceiving and running innovative high-level events to leverage sales, as well as running content creation business enterprises.

Our approach to business and teaching has been recognised academically and within the publishing industry. We have been awarded Best Newcomer at the Independent Publishing Guild Awards (2019) and a *Times* Higher Education Award for Excellence and Innovation in the Arts (2018).

As our business continues to grow, so too does the experience our students have upon entering UCLan Publishing.

To find out more, please visit
www.uclanpublishing.com/courses/

Studying the Novel